Growing Up in the Great Depression

by Richard Wormser

Illustrated with photographs

ATHENEUM 1994 • *New York*

MAXWELL MACMILLAN CANADA • *Toronto*

MAXWELL MACMILLAN INTERNATIONAL • *New York Oxford Singapore Sydney*

To Ellen, with love

Many of the quoted interviews were conducted directly by the author or came from original letters and interviews, some of which were written to President Roosevelt (now on file at the Roosevelt Archives in Hyde Park). Others were collected by various federal and state agencies (e.g., CCC, Department of Labor), from university students conducting research on the depression, or from former government workers.

Atheneum
Macmillan Publishing Company
866 Third Avenue
New York, NY 10022

Maxwell Macmillan Canada, Inc.
1200 Eglinton Avenue East
Suite 200
Don Mills, Ontario M3C 3N1

Macmillan Publishing Company is part of the Maxwell Communication Group of Companies.
First edition
Printed in the United States of America
10 9 8 7 6 5 4 3 2 1
The text of this book is set in Garamond 3.
Book design by Blake Logan

Library of Congress Cataloging-in-Publication Data
Wormser, Richard, date.
Growing up in the Great Depression / by Richard Wormser : illustrated with photographs. — 1st ed.
p. cm.
Includes bibliographical references and index.
Summary: Historical background, interviews, and photographs combine to provide an impression of childhood during the Great Depression.
ISBN 0-689-31711-5
1. United States—Social life and customs—1918–1945— Juvenile literature. 2. Depressions—1929—United States—Juvenile literature. 3. United States—Economic conditions—1918–1945—Juvenile literature. 4. Youth—United States—History—20th century—Juvenile literature. [1. United States—Social life and customs—1918–1945. 2. Depressions—1929. 3. United States—Economic conditions—1918–1945.] I. Title.
E169.W79 1994
973.91—dc20 93-20686

Contents

February 1936

Mr. and Mrs. Roosevelt
Wash., D.C.

Dear Mr. President,

I'm a boy of 12 years. I want to tell you about my family. My father hasn't worked for about 5 months. He went plenty of times to relief, he filled out application. They won't give us anything. I don't know why. Please do something. We haven't paid four months rent. Everyday the landlord rings the bell, we don't open the door for him. We are afraid that we'll be put out. Been put out before and don't want it to happen again. Haven't paid the gas bill and electric bill, haven't paid the grocery bill in three months. My brother goes to Lane Tech High School. He's 18 years old and hasn't gone in 2 weeks because he got no carfare. I have a sister, she's 20 years old, can't find work. My father, he staying home. All the time he's crying because he can't find work. I said why are you crying daddy and daddy said, why shouldn't I cry when there is nothing in the house. I feel sorry for him. That night I couldn't sleep. The next morning I write this letter to you, in my room. We're American citizens and were born in Chicago, Ill. and I don't know why they won't help us. Please answer right away because we need it. We'll starve. Thank you.

God bless you.

CHAPTER ONE

How It Began

In 1930 America went bust. A great economic depression settled over the country like a plague, afflicting the rich and the poor, men, women, and children, black and white, foreign- and native-born, workers and farmers. Millions of people lost their jobs, their businesses, their farms, their homes, their savings, and their self-respect.

It all seemed to happen suddenly. For ten years the country seemed to be on a spending spree. In 1920, 7.5 million automobiles had been purchased. By 1929 there were 26.5 million. The sales of goods rose from $4.9 billion in 1920 to $7.06 billion in 1929. Industry was booming. From 1925 to 1929, the number of factories increased from 183,877 to 206,663. More high school students were graduating than ever before (from 16 percent in 1920 to 28 percent in 1930).

With money came the pursuit of pleasure. The 1920s were a decade of fads: the crossword puzzle, golf, and a Chinese game called Mah-Jongg. Everybody seemed to be out for a good time. The dance crazes were the Charleston and the Black Bottom. People flocked to

The people with their hands in the air are buying and selling stocks. When the stock market crashed everyone was selling but nobody was buying, and prices dropped.

the theater to watch glamorous shows and show girls. And while it was illegal to buy or sell liquor (a constitutional amendment had been passed in 1918 that banned alcoholic beverages), there was plenty of "booze" around. The gangsters and bootleggers made sure of that. Al Capone and "Bugs" Moran owned Chicago, Dutch Schultz and Arnold Rothstein ruled New York, the Purple Gang controlled Detroit, while Joe Kennedy, the father of the future president of the United States, was a major bootleg liquor dealer in Boston. Not only did bootleggers supply people with liquor, they supplied the places in which to drink it. They opened clubs and speakeasies where you could dance, drink, and often gamble without fear of arrest because the police had been paid off. It was no wonder preachers were warning that America was on the road to hell. They were far more accurate than most people gave them credit for.

The index of America's prosperity was Wall Street and the stock market. From the end of World War I in 1919 stock prices kept rising. In 1924, the average price of the twenty-five leading industrial stocks in America was $120 a share. By 1929, the same stocks were worth $542. Many people believed they had found a money machine that could not fail. Everybody knew somebody—or so they said—who had bought a stock at $10 one day and sold it for $20 the next. And the person who bought it for $20 sold it for $50—and so on down the line. It seemed as if prosperity would last forever. One of the famous millionaires of the day, Jacob Raskob, remarked, "Not only can one be rich, but one ought to be rich."

Despite the fact that millions were being made on the stock market, most Americans lacked money to invest. Out of the then 27.5 million families in America, 21.5 million of them earned under $3,000 a year, and, of those, 6 million families earned less than $1,000.

Yet advertising told them that they too had a role to play in the general prosperity. They were urged to buy the goods and services the society was producing. Most people bought, but many couldn't afford to pay the full price all at once. Instead, they bought on credit. They bought cars on credit, clothes on credit, houses on credit, furniture on credit, radios on credit. And the more goods they bought, the more were manufactured for them to buy, and the higher the stock market rose.

But underneath the glitter, there were distinct rumblings of an economic earthquake, and many of the "big boys"—which was what the newspapers called the most influential business leaders—knew it. Publicly, they were making statements declaring the stock market to be solid and urging people to buy stocks and invest in America. Privately they were selling all the stocks they owned. The insiders knew that many businesses were having hard times. Despite the seeming prosperity, unemployment in certain industries was high, farm prices were low, and stocks were selling for much more than they were worth. Even Herbert Hoover, who was then president of the United States, knew it. But the stock market was riding on a speeding roller coaster and the president's men were afraid that if they tried to control it, the roller coaster would fly off the tracks and injure a lot of people. So they did nothing, hoping that everything would work itself out.

On October 24, 1929, the roller coaster finally crashed. Stock prices plummeted. The more desperate people were to get rid of their stocks, the lower prices fell. On that one day, the value of stocks fell fourteen billion dollars. Everybody wanted to sell, but nobody wanted to buy. There seemed to be no end to the slide. Prices for stocks and bonds dropped hour by hour. Thousands of small investors watched the stock market quotations appear on the ticker tape, the numbers lower each time they passed by. People crowded around radio rooms on ocean liners, in newspaper offices, and made long distance calls one after another to hear the news. On the floor of the stock exchange, there was total confusion and then panic. Brokers physically battled one another to compete for the few buyers available. They pulled one another's hair, bit, punched, and shoved in order to make a sale—and at any price. A messenger boy who happened to be at the stock exchange by chance offered a bid of one dollar as a joke for shares in White Sewing Machine and wound up owning ten thousand shares of stock in the company.

The captains of industry and finance as well as President Hoover kept making public statements that the crash was temporary. But prices continued to fall. Within a year, the sale of railroad and utility bonds dropped from $10 billion to $1 billion. The average income per person dropped from $847 a year to $465. Millions of investors were financially ruined, losing everything they owned. They had bought stocks on margin, which meant that they actually paid for only a small part of the stock's value and owed the rest, assuming they could pay it off as the stock price rose. Now they were being called to put up the rest of the money. They exhausted their savings, sold their wives' jewelry, borrowed from friends and relatives, trying to raise cash to cover their losses. It was like throwing money down a bottomless well.

A few committed suicide. When the president of a cigar company saw the value of stock in his company drop from $113.50 to $4 a share in a single day, he rented a hotel room, climbed out on the ledge, and, despite the efforts of a waiter to drag him back inside, jumped to his death. Another man, having lost all his money and owing hundreds of thousands, shot himself. His dying words were, "Tell the boys I can't pay." Many who killed themselves did so because the crash exposed their illegal dealings. Bank presidents were caught using customers' money to play the market. Rumors of suicides became so exaggerated that when a man was spotted working on a roof of a building, a crowd gathered to see if he would jump. In a few tragic cases, ruined men went home and killed their families before killing themselves. The economic lights had gone out and there was darkness throughout the land.

What caused the Great Depression? Some said the wealth of the country was badly distributed: too many rich people and too many poor. The top 5 percent of the country owned 33 percent of all the real wealth. The 27,400 wealthiest families had as much money as the 12 million poorest families. The poor had no money to buy goods and services, so after a while there were too many products on the market and not enough people to buy them. The taxes on imports from other countries were so high that foreigners couldn't sell their goods here and make money to pay their debts to the United States. In addition, the foundations on which many businesses were built were shaky. Many companies' stock had risen to a lot more than the companies were really worth. At the first tremors, these firms went broke. It was like a snowball rolling downhill, getting bigger and rolling faster every second. When the companies went broke, so did the banks that had lent them money. Workers who lost their jobs couldn't pay their bills. The businesses that depended upon them also went under because they didn't have enough customers to survive. When the snowball finally came to a stop, there was one vast heap of ruined companies, ruined factories, ruined banks, and ruined human lives. A nurse in Tucson, Arizona, wrote:

> I retired one night safe and independent with $7852.00 in the bank and awoke the next morning with $12.00 in my purse. Like so many others, I lost all my savings in a bank failure.

And a man in Florida wrote the president:

> Is there no department to take care of the injustice done to me who bought stocks instead of a home? Mine was not paper money but hard earned dollars. I have worked hard and long and now I have not enough money to pay a necessary dentist's bill. I was born with a sense of justice and now it has been outraged.

In October 1931, two years after the collapse of the stock market, 9,378,000 workers were unemployed. In December, 10,814,000 were out of work. In January of 1932, unemployment grew to 11,500,000. In March, it rose to 12,000,000 and in June, 13,000,000. By December it was 13,587,000. In January 1933 it reached 14,597,000, and in March, when Franklin Delano Roosevelt was inaugurated as president of the United States, unemployment had reached 15,071,000. In some cities, 80 percent of the work force was without jobs. At the lowest point in the depression, 34 million men, women, and children were without income, 28 percent of the

American people. Factories were working at 15 percent of capacity, if they were working at all. More than 6,000 banks went bankrupt, one-quarter of the nation's banks; 85,000 businesses had failed. The price of wheat dropped from $1.09 to 39 cents a bushel. Farmers in the Midwest burned their crops and poured milk onto the highways to protest the fact that the prices they would receive from selling the food was far less than the cost of raising and transporting it.

Hundreds of thousands of people were evicted from their homes and farms and lived in tents and shacks made of cardboard, tar paper, scrap wood, or metal. Fewer people got married and fewer children were born. By 1932, more than a million children were not receiving an education because there was no money to pay teachers. Some schools were operating only three days a week and others closed ten

The only help for many of those who lost their jobs was charity provided by city and religious organizations.

In 1932, despite the fact that many people blamed President Herbert Hoover for the depression, he ran for reelection. Hoover was nominated by the Republican party even though most of the delegates felt he didn't have a chance to win.

months of the year. There was some relief for the needy from local governments and charities, but to be eligible, people had to sell their possessions, including their home, and cancel their life insurance. Some states would not allow people on relief to vote and some churches banned families on relief from attending services. There was talk of revolution in the air. Hitler had come to power in Germany, and there were those who admired him. Stalin was in power in the Soviet Union, and there were those who believed that he had the answer.

People turned their eyes and hopes to the government for help. The president, Herbert Hoover, was an able administrator, but he lacked compassion. He believed that the federal government shouldn't interfere in the crisis, that depressions were natural and normal under capitalism, and that things would soon get better. "The traditional business of the country is . . . on a sound and prosperous basis," he said. When a few thousand World War I veterans peacefully marched to Washington to pressure Congress to give them a bonus promised to them for 1945, Hoover used federal troops against them. The soldiers drove the veterans out with bayonets and tanks and burned their makeshift homes, even though the demonstrators were unarmed. When farmers and workers sought economic help from the government, Hoover denied it to them. He did, however, make money available to certain big businesses to keep them afloat. People were so angry with him that they called the colonies

Hoover's opponent was the governor of New York, Franklin D. Roosevelt, who defeated him in a landslide.

of makeshift houses built by the homeless "Hoovervilles" as an expression of their contempt for the president. By 1932 it had become clear that Herbert Hoover was no longer the American people's choice for the job.

The man the people turned to was Franklin Delano Roosevelt. One-time vice presidential candidate, former governor of New York, crippled by polio and confined to a wheelchair, Roosevelt was a man of remarkable spirit and temperament. In spite of being a nephew of former president Theodore Roosevelt and born to a life of wealth and privilege, Roosevelt had an intuitive empathy with most of the American people. He inspired them and gave them hope. In turn, they loved and trusted him, and in their despair turned to him for salvation.

Elected by a landslide in 1932, Roosevelt set the tone of his administration in his inauguration speech in March of 1933. As the nation listened to him over the radio, he spoke the following words of inspiration:

> Let me first assert my firm belief that the only thing we have to fear is fear itself. Nameless, unreasoning, unjustified terror which paralyzes needed efforts to convert retreat into advance.

But despite Roosevelt's speech and his policies, which would profoundly change the relationship between the federal government and the people, the depression lasted ten long, hard years.

Children were especially affected. The Republicans under Hoover refused to recognize how much they were suffering. As hundreds of children were dying of malnutrition, Hoover's secretary of the interior, Ray Lynn Williams, infuriated a group of social workers when he told them, "Our children are apt to profit rather than suffer from what is going on. Children receive better care and more suitable food . . . than in past good times." A social worker in Chicago indirectly responded to this callous remark when she noted:

> The load of suffering falls so definitely on the children. They are cold and hungry, lacking security and developing physical conditions sure to bring on tuberculosis . . . and mental attitudes to bring on delinquency. We are terribly upset because of the [recent] death of a child . . . due to the inadequate food ration given to the family. . . .

For many children, the depression meant their childhood ended early. It meant a life of picking cotton or working in a factory ten hours a day instead of going to school or playing. For others, it meant pretending nothing was wrong so the neighbors wouldn't know their father was broke or on the verge of suicide. It meant not being able to call a doctor when you were sick, not having the heat of a fire when you were cold, not having food when you were hungry. One child remembered:

> We didn't have anything to eat for a whole week but potatoes. . . . My brother went around to the grocery store and got them to give him meat for his dog—only he didn't have any dog. We ate that dog meat with the potatoes.

For millions of children, the Great Depression meant not having clothes for school, making sweaters out of old grain sacks, and wearing cardboard in their shoes to cover the holes. Sometimes it meant listening to their parents scream at each other, watching their father beaten down because he couldn't find a job, seeing their mother age under the strain. Or it meant moving every three months to a new place because there wasn't money to pay the rent.

During the depression children were able to endure many hardships, but the hardest of all was to be separated from their families. Alma Meyer, who was then ten, watched her father slowly deteriorate. She was the middle child of a family of five who had lived a simple but comfortable middle-class life in Toledo, Ohio, before the crash.

My father had worked 20 years as a salesman, and when he was laid off, he said we weren't to worry, he would have another job in no time. We had some money saved away and we owned our own home and had a car, and daddy was an optimist and always left home and returned home with a smile. Every day, he would get up and put on his best suit and shirt and tie and leave at 6 o'clock in the morning to look for a job. "The early bird catches the worm," he said. About 6 o'clock in the evening he'd come home looking tired, but cheerful and tell us that no, there was nothing today, but they had liked him wherever he went—he could tell that—and they would call him the first opening they had. He used to go into every building and knock on every door of every office, but it was always the same story. Nobody was hiring. Everybody was laying off. Nobody knew how long they would be in business. And I used to watch my father get more tired every day, and his spirits get a little bit lower. Although he was a salesman all his life, he started looking for work in factories as a laborer. When he heard there might be a job somewhere, he would get up at two, three in the morning, sometimes the day before so he could be the first on line. But no matter how early he went, there'd always be people at the factory gate before him. And he never got hired. We children used to be afraid that the family would be broken up and we'd be sent away. We had heard of children being sent to live somewhere else because their folks couldn't afford to keep them. So we'd try to be extra good so we wouldn't be sent away. I remember I didn't want to make any noise because I was scared that if my parents heard me, they'd know I was there and they might send me away, where if I was real quiet maybe they would forget about me and I wouldn't have to go. But eventually, mom and dad shipped us kids to live with relatives. They said it was a holiday and we'd all be back together again soon. I went to live with my grandparents. I cried the night

> I left. I told my parents that if they kept me, I'd eat only one meal a day so they could save money. I was so angry with my dad, even though it wasn't his fault. He tried so hard, but the depression was too much. It broke his spirit. It broke my child's heart, I can tell you that.

For some children, the signs of poverty weren't all that obvious. Russell Baker, who grew up to be a columnist for the *New York Times,* remembered in his autobiography, *Growing Up*:

> If anyone told me we were poor, I would have been astounded. We ate well enough. There was always a bowl of oatmeal at breakfast, a bologna sandwich for lunch, and a cup of coffee with which to wash it down. For supper, the standard menu was chipped beef gravy on bread or macaroni and cheese. Canned salmon was 11 cents a can and a real treat.

The depression did bring many families closer, when they worked together to soften the harsh effects of hard times. For many children, the depression made them stronger. If their families were too poor to buy toys, they invented games and made dolls out of corncobs and broomsticks. If they only had meat once a month, then that day was turned into a holiday as each child eagerly awaited his or her slice of meat, wondering, as they watched their father slice it, who would get the first piece and who would get the last. If it was too cold to sit in the house, they would snuggle under the covers of their beds. If they couldn't go to the movies, they read books or listened to their parents tell them stories. In farm areas, some children walked four or five miles to school each day or hitched up a horse and buggy and rode. They were proud that their mothers and fathers needed their help and proud that they could be of help, and often what they lacked materially, they gained spiritually.

"There's no question about it," Dale Gene Scales remembers. "We were poor, we did without, we were hungry a lot of times, but we survived because we stayed close as a family. That made all the difference."

Although from different backgrounds and circumstances, the men and women in this book shared one thing in common—all were growing up during the depression. Their ages ranged from ten to nineteen. Their experiences varied: they were hoboes and dancers, worked in sweatshops or farms, became poorer or richer, remained unemployed or became labor organizers, lived by their wits or went to jail. Each of them was shaped by the depression and in turn many of them helped shape the America that emerged from it. In the end, despite their adversities, they were survivors.

CHAPTER TWO

Hoboes

*B*ill saw the "shrimp" dart out from behind a pile of railroad ties and make straight for the slow-moving train. His first thought was that the kid was too short to reach the ladder on the side of the boxcar and he was probably too young to be hoboing in the first place. Some of the kids he was running into these days were as young as eleven or twelve. At seventeen, Bill began to feel old.

When Bill saw the shrimp headed for his boxcar, he reached out and offered a hand. The train was picking up speed and the shrimp had to run fast to keep up with it. He reached Bill's boxcar, grabbed his hand, and swung himself into the car. Bill was surprised at how light his new traveling companion was.

"Where to, Bo?"

"Up Idaho."

Bill instinctively exchanged the traditional hobo greeting before he realized that the shrimp was a girl. He had met a number of young girls hoboing on the road, but this was the first time he had met one who was traveling by herself. Usually it was too dangerous for girls to be alone on the road. But at the age of fifteen, Annie McLaren was a veteran and, despite her small size, able to take care of herself.

The year was 1934, and Bill and Annie were two of the 250,000 teenage hoboes wandering across America seeking work, adventure, escape, and freedom during the depression years. At home, they had names like Fred, Tom, Jack, Anne, Katy, and Bill. On the road they were known as Happy Joe and Blink, Lady Lou, Bust, Spit and Bo-Peep, Dressy and Peg-Leg Al, Dopey Jack, Candles, and Whistles. They often met by accident in a boxcar or jail, a mission house or hobo jungle, and stayed together for protection and friendship. They had left home because of the "big trouble"—which was what they called the Great Depression. Some were kicked out of their homes or asked to leave because there wasn't enough food for everybody. Some fled because they had trouble with their parents and the depression only made things worse. Others, like Bill Bailey, left on their own. Sixteen and in high school, Bill immediately dropped out of school to support his mother and seven brothers and sisters when the depression started.

> There was no work anywhere. Every time I sat down at the dinner table and saw how hungry my little brothers and sisters were, I felt I was snatching the food out of their mouths. I figured it would be better for everyone if I left home. There'd be more to eat and maybe I could earn some money and send it to my mom. I didn't intend to become a hobo. I was just looking for a job in another city. But since there wasn't any jobs to be had, I wound up bumming around the country. I became a hobo, although I always looked for work. So eventually, I began to ride the rails, jumping into boxcars. And they were filled with people. Thousands of them. Farmers, workers, people from all over—all

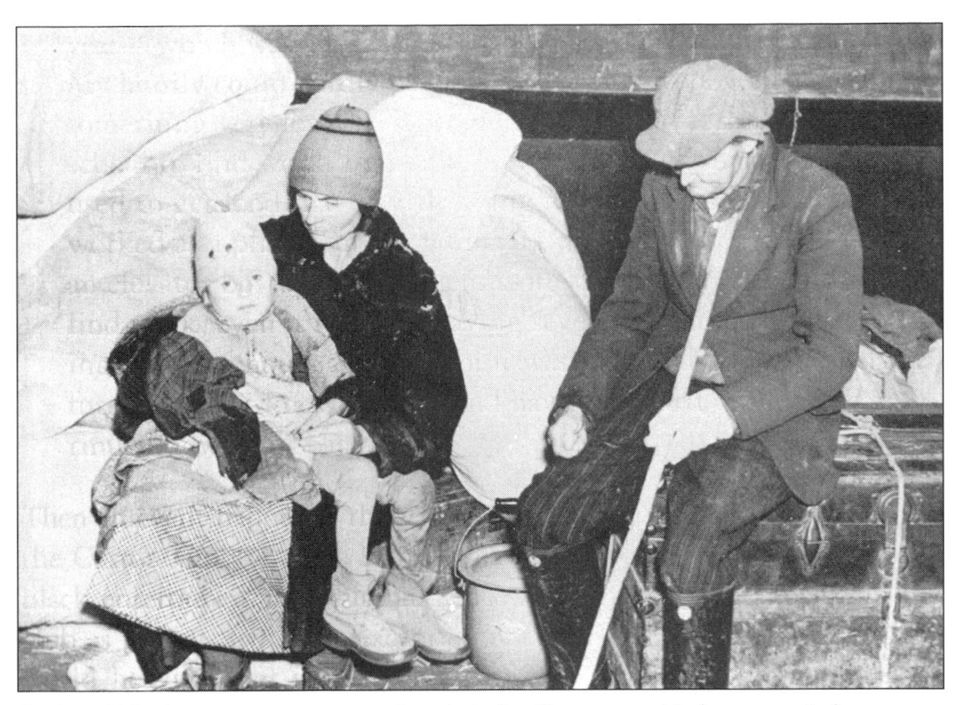

In the 1930s, it was not uncommon for whole families to travel in boxcars as hoboes.

of them like you were, going somewhere, looking for work. It was pretty obvious that most of them had been hard-working people. You could see it just by looking at them. Sometimes they would ride in reefer cars where they kept the chilled cargoes. They would get inside and button up to keep warm, throw a few rags around them. That's how bad things were. There were whole families riding together, mother, father, couple of kids. It was a phenomenal thing for me to see them—in their rags, laying in the car, kids with runny noses, crying. And there were kids, my age. Some younger. By themselves. There was nothing for them at home so they left. Boys and girls, some as young as 12. It was sad, but that's the way it was.

Life on the road might have seemed romantic at first, but it was often difficult and dirty. One young man who later became a congressman wrote of his life as a hobo.

> I slept in hobo jungles, got lousy and got preached and lectured at by four flushing racketeers who called themselves preachers. I saw enough to make anyone sick for a long time. I saw one mother and father sleeping on the wet ground with a baby in between wrapped in sacks. There was promiscuity, filth, degradation. Men and families slept in jails, railroad urinals, dugouts and tumbled-down shacks.

These two pictures show what it was like to catch a ride on a train. In the first photo, the man is riding in a boxcar. In the second, men are "decking" the train, that is, riding on top.

Young people had to watch out for brakemen in the rail yards and police everywhere else. But worst of all were the "wolves"—older hoboes who preyed on the young, forcing them to beg, cook their meals, wash their clothes, and sometimes provide sexual favors. The only real safety for young people was to travel in groups.

Travel was a big part of a young hobo's life. Some hitchhiked, but hitchhiking was a solitary game and dangerous. Most traveled by train. A few traveled for the love of traveling. They were loners, called "passenger stiffs," who would ride on passenger trains, the fastest and most dangerous trains of all. These trains had no boxcars, so hoboes rode underneath on the carriage upon which the cars rested, on the roof, or on the "blind"—a section of the baggage car that wasn't used. Passenger stiffs rode for the thrill of riding and not for travel. Some froze to death on the roofs of the trains when they crossed over the mountains. Some slid off and fell underneath the wheels. It was the price many were willing to pay for belonging to a very exclusive club.

But for the majority of young hoboes in the 1930s the freight train was their main means of transportation. Friendly brakemen would sometimes allow them to climb into a boxcar before the train started. But when the brakemen were tough or mean, the youths had to steal aboard the train after it started. Bill Bailey recalled that some brakemen would beat you if you got caught on their trains:

> Some of these brakemen would bash your fingers or break your knee so you couldn't jump on their trains. There was one guy who carried a baseball bat—they used to call him Bat Branigan. He asked no questions. He'd just belt you with the bat.

Stealing aboard a train while it was moving required skills that not everybody had. Thousands of people were killed or maimed trying to do it. The overall statistics for death and injuries during the first four years of the depression were grim. For one railroad alone, the Missouri Pacific, the figures were as follows: in 1929, 103 people killed, 156 injured; in 1930, 114 killed, 221 injured; in 1931, 125 killed, 247 injured; in 1932, 91 killed, 214 injured. Overall 433 people were killed and 838 injured. Bill Bailey recalls the risks:

> It was dangerous riding the rails. You had to know what you were doing. You couldn't just walk onto a train like you was a passenger. You had to jump on as the train was moving. If you tried to jump on when it was going too fast, you could fall under the wheels. Same with jumping off. You could break your neck if the train hadn't slowed down enough. When you was inside, you had to learn how to sleep. If you got too close to the bulkhead or was sitting in an open door and the train suddenly stopped, you could get your head smashed or even cut off.

The best time to board a moving train was when it was traveling slowly through the yard. When hoboes saw the brakeman give the engineer the signal to start, and the train lurched forward, its boxcars and gondolas buckling and banging against one another, they would dash out from their hiding places behind piles of railroad ties, stored boxes, and idle trains and run for the train like racehorses breaking from a gate. The oldest and strongest youths would swing on board first and then help pull others up. Some were boosted aboard from the ground. As long as the train moved slowly everyone could keep up by walking alongside. But as it picked up speed, those who had not boarded had to jog to keep up. As the train picked up more speed, the young hoboes ran faster. If someone stumbled he would desperately scramble to his feet to keep up, often risking serious injury or death. For many young hoboes, being left behind was far worse than being injured.

When teenagers on the road weren't riding from one place to another, they were usually hustling for food. In an average day, a

Some people walked and hitchhiked across the country, seeking work as they went.

young panhandler would walk twenty miles in an eight-hour period, asking for food and money. Most of the time, the teenagers were hungry. They thought about food throughout the day, talked about it in the evening, and dreamed of it at night. To get food they would spend eight hours a day "on the stem"—slang for panhandling on the street. Some worked restaurants, groceries, butcher stores, and bakeries. Others begged people on the street for money. In those days, you could buy a full dinner for a quarter. In the countryside, young hoboes would go from farm to farm. One young hobo explained that when he did that he would wrap extra protection around his legs and put some heavy rocks in his pocket in case the farmer set his dog upon him. Bill Bailey remembered how fierce the competition for food could be:

> I went to one lady's house in some God forsaken place in South Dakota. As soon as I knocked on the front door, I heard someone knocking on the back door. And I could hear the woman inside talking to someone saying, "I'll get the front door first." And she came to me and said, "What is it? Hurry up because someone's at the back door." And I said, "Lady, all I want is a sandwich if you could spare it. I just got off a freight car and I'm headed west." She tells me to wait a second so she can answer the back door and I can hear this kid asking her if she can give him something to eat. So here's this poor woman, being hit at both ends of the house. And the sad part was that all she had was bread. And she says to each of us in turn. "All I can help you with is a loaf of bread. I can't give you no meat. I have no butter." I says o.k., I'll take the bread. So we both took the bread.

Sometimes a young hobo would get lucky and eat like a king. Farmers tended to be more generous with food, especially if they had had a good crop. Also, many people were more likely to respond to the plea of a young person. One thirteen-year-old hobo remembered that he approached one family for a few apples and wound up with "half a chicken, a ham and egg sandwich, a quart of milk and—would you believe it—a piece of homemade pie. [A piece of pie was the ultimate dream of every hobo.] When I left they gave me a loaf of bread, cookies, a couple of bottles of homemade jelly, and all the apples I could stuff in my pockets."

A straightforward approach to begging did not always work. People became hardened because there were so many hoboes on the road. Young hoboes often developed a "front" of some sort, usually a story about a sick brother, a dying mother, the need to get to the next town. Some children panhandled by pretending they had deformities and diseases. When nothing worked, many stole. They became experts at stealing chickens from henhouses, fruit from orchards, vegetables from grocery trucks, and milk from doorsteps. However, there was a code of honor among many of the younger hoboes that you could steal only to survive and not for profit.

If there were only a few young people together, they would often head to a hobo camp, or "jungle," for something to eat and a place to sleep. Bill Bailey, who tended to travel with one or two others, chose the camps.

> The camps were often the best place for a hobo to hang out, although they could be real dangerous at times. They attracted some tough characters who would pull a knife on you and hold you up. Since I didn't have anything, I didn't worry too much. But most of the guys were like me. They were all hungry. All looking for jobs. All trying to keep out of jail.
>
> One of the rules of the camp was that in order to partake of food, you had to bring some. Most camps had a kettle going all day and night and whatever food people brought got thrown in. I always tried to pick up some potatoes or carrots from a grocery store or some bones from the butcher. After you ate, you sat around and talked. Guys would tell where they had been and what sheriffs to watch out for, what bad experiences they had.

If a group of young hoboes was large enough, it would make its own camp. Once in a while, someone managed to "find" a small pig or a chicken and it would wind up on the barbecue. In many groups, there were one or two teenagers who had grown up on a farm and knew how to slaughter animals. Other times the meals were little more than flavored boiling water. It all depended upon the luck of the day.

After dinner the young hoboes would sit around and talk and tell each other of their adventures that day or their life stories. They had developed their own language and a conversation might go like this.

Many unemployed men became tramps, traveling around the country on freight trains, and living in hobo jungles or camps.

> "I was on the Fritz see. And I carries the banner slinking harness-bulls. Until glims. Then I batters private plunging like a gandy dancer and red bull socks into the old heavy foot himself. 'Tooting ringers for a scoffing,' he says. 'Come with me, I'll give you a scoffing.' Skating on my uppers, I mush talks him out of a hustle buggy ride into mongee."

Which translated meant:

> "I was broke. All night I walked the streets avoiding cops in uniform until dawn. Then I began begging door to door when, without warning, I run into a detective. 'Are you begging for something to eat? Come with me I'll get you something.' I was able to convince him not to call the squad car but to feed me."

If things got really bad, and there was little or no food to be had, there was always one place where a hobo could get a meal—the missions. There were large missions like the "Sallies"—the Salvation Army, usually found in cities, and many smaller missions in small towns. But a hobo usually had to listen to a sermon and usually do several hours' work for a meal. Both of these requirements were resented by most young people. Mission food was usually pretty bad, too. Often it was just beans and stew. According to many hoboes, the amount of meat in the stew was small enough to be hidden behind a single bean.

There were also free meals at public relief centers or shelters run by local government agencies. The food varied depending on the agency, but many places offered little more than a thin, watery vegetable soup, some stale bread, peanut butter or bologna sandwiches, and coffee and stale doughnuts. It could be dangerous too. A lot of desperate people hung out at shelters. One man remembered:

> We was sitting and eating and this kid had a lot of bread piled up on his plate. He was a little kid. Suddenly, this big, burly lumberjack type reached over and grabbed all the kid's bread in his huge hand and began to stuff it in his mouth. The kid reached into his pocket and drew out a pocket knife and run it right into the guy's hand, making him drop the bread. But before the kid could pick it up, twenty guys hit the floor on their hands and knees, stuffing it in their mouths before the kid could get any. And the lumberjack was crying about how the kid had stabbed him.

Getting food was easy compared to getting clothes. Many of the teenagers who hit the road during the depression left home with only the clothes they were wearing. Within weeks, the garments began to fall apart. The young people soon became expert at repairs, using old bones for needles, newspapers for lining and underwear, rubber tires for shoes, and grain sacks for sweaters. One teenager nicknamed Dressy managed to wear a suit, shirt, tie, and hat every day, covering them at night with handkerchiefs to protect them.

In the wintertime, the biggest problems were getting shoes and overcoats—especially when the weather was freezing. The youths wrapped their feet with old newspapers, many pairs of socks, pieces of rubber and wool—whatever they could find to protect them from getting frostbitten. Bill Bailey had his own source of clothes:

> I learned that the best way to get clothes was to go to people who had clothes and one of the guys that had clothes was the undertaker. I'd go knock at the door and ask, "Hey anything lying around?" You know, because they probably had undressed the stiff and the clothes were there and sometimes the family didn't want them anyway.

Most young hoboes preferred to sleep outdoors when the weather was warm. They would lie on the ground at night, or on a piece of cloth or newspaper, their undernourished bodies attacked by mosquitoes, sand fleas, lice, and ants. Some built lean-tos for protection against the rain, or makeshift tents; others settled in caves, although there was the fear that dangerous animals might also live in them.

During cold weather, a hobo could sleep either in a hobo jungle or at a shelter. Both had their dangers. In a jungle, there was always a risk of someone robbing you or a drunk throwing up on you. Rats were attracted to the jungles because there was so much debris and they would scamper over sleeping bodies. Girls were especially vulnerable to rape in a camp. Some girls did work as prostitutes to earn money from time to time, but few thought of themselves as professionals. For them, it was just a way to survive. If someone got sick, he or she would wind up in the charity ward of a hospital. Many

A view of a jail from behind the bars. Many hoboes were glad to spend a night in jail, where they could sleep in a warm place and count on at least one free meal.

young people feared going there because there was a rumor that charity cases were given the "black bottle." This was supposed to contain poison to kill them quickly and save the state money. Many people did die in the hospitals, usually because they arrived at the hospital too sick to be helped.

The greatest danger to a hobo was the police. While most young hoboes had a story of being helped by a nice cop who let him or her stay in jail for a few days (many hoboes preferred to spend the night in jail; it was free room and board), they also had many horror stories of police brutality. The local police often took the law into their own hands when it came to hoboes and might beat and arrest them and, at times, put them on the chain gang—the prison work squad—without a trial. Bill Bailey remembers two sheriffs he encountered:

> There was this one town I went to and when I started to ask for something to eat, the guy told me to go to the sheriff's office. He said all the merchants had made a donation to city hall and the sheriff was giving out free food. So we went down to the sheriff's office and asked for our dinner. "What dinner?" he said. When we explained what the merchant said, he locked us up overnight without giving us anything to eat. He was pocketing the money for himself. The next day, he marched us out of town. We had to stand in the hot sun for four hours before the next freight stopped. When the train arrived, that lousy sheriff told us to get into one of the box cars. It turned out to be a cattle car that stunk to high heaven. When we protested, he pointed his gun at us and said, "*Get in there!!*" So we got inside this stinking mess and he warned us never to show our faces in his town again—which of course we didn't.
>
> Then there was this other sheriff by the name of "Kickem" Packston. He used to walk into a hobo camp and kick over everything he saw standing. He would kick over the stew, the coffee, he'd kick you if you were lying on the ground. Well one day he sneaks up on this jungle camp and he sees two guys standing over a little fire with a pot, and he thought they were making a slumgullion—that's what we used to call a hobo stew. So he walked right up to it and without saying a word, he kicked it over. The next thing you know, he was blown to bits. So were the two guys who were stirring it and half the camp was destroyed. It seems these guys were a couple of safecrackers and they were boiling down nitroglycerin and when he kicked it, the nitro exploded and blew him up. None of us shed a tear about it, I can tell you that.

While the police generally disliked hoboes and often ran them out of town, they were particularly vicious toward black hoboes. Many were beaten, wrongly arrested, imprisoned, and sentenced to hard labor; some were killed. Yet blacks were generally accepted in hobo camps. While there was discrimination, life on the road tended to break down some of the racial barriers that existed in America during this period.

In the end, as the depression eased, many young hoboes returned to mainstream society, got jobs, and raised families. They knew that if they stayed too long on the road, they would waste their lives drifting from one place to another. As the years went by, many forgot much of the pain and fear and misery of being a hobo and remembered the friendships, adventures, and good times. For Bill Bailey, who eventually became a merchant seaman, his days as a teenage hobo taught him much about life. The one thing that he never forgot, he says, is the people he met and the humanity he found.

> I had just gotten off of a box car after having ridden for three days and I was dying of thirst and I stopped at the first house I saw and asked for a glass of water. There was this lady there who lived with her kid and she fed me and gave me milk to drink and I did some chores for her. I must have looked pretty bad for I remember her saying, "Oh Son, you're in an awful mess. Stay here a few minutes and I'll see if I can get you some clothes." And she comes back a few minutes later with her twelve-year-old son, who's a big kid, carrying a jacket, and the kid is saying "But Mom, that's my favorite jacket." And she says, "Son, this boy needs it more than you do." And she gives it to me. It was phenomenal how sometimes people would open up their hearts to you.

CHAPTER THREE

Dust

The problem was the sunshine.

From sunrise to sunset, the skies were clear blue from one end of the horizon to the other. Like a lost lamb that had strayed from the flock, an occasional single soft white cloud would wander casually across the sky.

The weather was a picnicker's dream, but a farmer's nightmare. For blue skies meant another day without rain, and without rain there would be no crops. Beginning in 1930, and continuing for almost ten years, the farmers of the Midwest, including the plains states of North and South Dakota, Colorado, Kansas, Texas, Minnesota, Nebraska, and Oklahoma, saw little but blue skies—except when they turned brown and black, as great dust storms roared over the land.

When the Great Depression began, many farmers did not feel its effects too severely. They did not lose money in the stock market, because they had no money to invest. Unlike their city cousins, farmers had not prospered during the 1920s. Food prices had remained low while the cost of everything else was high. Because of this, farmers were burdened with debt. They had been forced to mortgage their homes, their land, their livestock, and sometimes their crops to buy their new farm machinery. By 1930, farmers were barely able to survive. A farmer needed at least $1,300 a year to get by—$900 of which went to pay for machinery and gasoline. By growing their own food and making their own clothes, the average farm family managed to keep their heads above water, but barely.

A reporter for the *Nation* magazine caught this mood when he wrote in 1931,

> On small farm after small farm anxious men and women were wondering how they were going to "get by." . . . If they can just "get by" until spring, if they can just "get by" and make another crop; if it will only be a good crop year and prices will only be a little better so they can get through . . . they will be satisfied. Gone are any thoughts of new cars, new clothes, new radios; the farmers are thinking in terms of food and feed for family and stock.

The depression sent many farmers over the edge. As prices for their crops dropped and the pressures from their debts increased, they began to rebel. To call national attention to their plight, they began to destroy food. The most famous of these protests was the Sioux City Milk Wars in September 1932. Two thousand farmers camped out along the nine highways leading to Sioux City, Iowa, set up barricades, and used planks with nails in them or pitchforks to blow out the tires of trucks carrying milk. They dumped thousands of gallons of milk on the ground rather than let it be brought to market, although they allowed deliveries to hospitals and to needy families. Most of the time the protest was peaceful. Eventually the police broke up the protest and arrested its leaders, but a compromise was reached with the farmers on price.

Then drought spread over most of the Midwest. Combined with the depression, it devastated the farmers. It wasn't all nature's fault. For years the farmers had helped to ruin their land by planting wheat on it every year instead of rotating crops to keep the soil healthy. Wheat was a cash crop for the plains farmer as cotton was a cash crop for the southern farmer; and in good times, both could be sold for high prices. But the price the farmers paid for overplanting was that they destroyed their land by removing the prairie grass that covered and protected the soil. In 1930 alone, it took a hundred tons of water a day to irrigate a one-hundred acre farm. And most of this water came from rain.

What does a drought do to the land when the moisture in the earth evaporates into the sky and there is no rain to replace it? The

A farmer boy looks at his land after several years of drought. Millions of acres of land were destroyed in the Midwest by the lack of rain.

sun burns down on the earth day after day until the ground becomes hot enough to burn your feet or cook your dinner—and then the land blisters and cracks open. The grass beneath your feet crunches as if you're walking over broken glass. Spring comes, but the trees and the bushes are leafless. Then the summer comes and with it the heat. It was said that in parts of Texas people went to hell for their vacation so they could cool off. In the summer of 1934 in Nebraska, the temperature reached 121 degrees. In Iowa, it reached 115. In Illinois, temperatures continued over 100 degrees for so long that four hundred people died from the heat. One man moved into his refrigerator and had to be treated for frostbite.

The heat was followed by grasshoppers. They ate what little wheat and corn was left, and then began to eat the washing on the line and the curtains in the house. There were grasshoppers in the fields, in the barns, and in the houses. If you opened a tin of sugar, grasshoppers would jump out. If you went to the bathroom or crawled into bed, you'd find them hopping there. One woman remarked that the grasshoppers had eaten everything on her farm but the fence posts. The next day, she reported the grasshoppers had eaten them too. But the worst was yet to come. The heat and the dead land and the grasshoppers and the depression were only the prelude to the biggest disaster of them all.

When the land is without water, when all the natural grasses have been destroyed, when the land has been overfarmed, then the rich topsoil turns to dust, loose and blowing in the wind. It might not have mattered all that much if the dust had stayed put. And if there had been good soil left, the dust might not have moved around very much. But when there was no longer anything to hold the dust down, it began to blow with the wind. Most of the time, the winds blew slowly and steadily out of the Southwest and piled dirt everywhere. Hour after hour, day after day, year after year, sand rattled against the windows and against the doors, leaving a fine powder

A "black blizzard" or dust storm appears over Big Spring, Texas, in the 1930s. These dust storms appeared throughout the Great Plains during the depression.

over everything—food, furniture, people's faces. It covered the cattle and the fields, the wild animals and the machinery. It blanketed the earth like snow and nothing escaped it. No matter how tightly a house was sealed, no matter how many rags were wedged around windows and doors, dust so thin it could not be seen by the eye entered the house and settled over everything. What was not blown about the earth was carried by the wind into the sky. It was a disaster waiting to happen. All the loose earth and dust needed was a high wind. And on May 9, 1934, the first of the high winds came.

There had been dust storms and sandstorms before May. But they were just hints of what was yet to come. On May 9, high-level winds sucked up the brown earth from Montana and Wyoming and then moved east, drawing more dirt as they went along. All together, some 350 million tons of dirt were carried along in the sky. And then, like some malignant Santa Claus distributing evil gifts, the wind dropped bundles of dirt as it blew. Twelve million tons of dust fell like snow on Chicago. Millions of tons were deposited on every city in its path from Cleveland, Ohio, to Buffalo, New York, and Atlanta, Georgia. When the storm finally blew out to sea, dust fell on the ships in the middle of the ocean.

This was the beginning. One year later, on April 14, 1935, the worst dust storm of all the depression years struck. Viola Cooper was then a teenager living on a farm in northern Oklahoma:

> We were at a prayer meeting at a neighbor's house—we didn't have a pastor or anything, and people couldn't go to Sunday school or a regular church—so we'd have prayer meeting at a neighbor's house. It started out to be a real beautiful spring day. It was mild and pleasant. I remember that because suddenly it began to get colder and colder. The temperature must of dropped thirty or forty degrees in a few hours. Birds were everywhere. They came flying in from the North and whirled around like they was crazy, twittering and shaking—they just wouldn't stay still. You couldn't see anything wrong in the sky, but you just felt something awful was going to happen. Just as we was getting near our house, we saw it. It looked like one of them tidal waves rolling in clear up to the top of the sky. At first, we thought it was a big old snow blizzard except it was black. We called it a black blizzard. It was just dirt way high in the air. It looked like the clouds had fallen to the ground. It was just pitiful. And when it hit the houses, no one could get their breath. You couldn't see a window in the house. All the chickens was out in our yard and when it hit them, it just covered them where they stood.
>
> It was a good thing we was close to home or we never would have made it. The dirt was so thick we couldn't see the radiator

> cap on the truck. If you walked in front of it, you couldn't tell that the headlights was on unless you put your face right next to them. People got lost in that blizzard and were buried in it. Children died. They'd get lost from their parents and wander around in circles rather than stay in one place until someone found them. This one little boy I heard about got himself stuck on a barbed wire fence, couldn't get loose and was buried over by the dirt. We tried to protect ourselves as best we could. People put wet clothes over themselves and the kids. But it was hard to protect anybody from that dirt.

Throughout the mid-thirties the dust storms swept over the plains states. Some towns were covered almost twenty-four hours a day with dust and darkness. Children were often terrified. Ella Wallin, who also grew up in Oklahoma, remembered that during one violent storm, one of her childhood friends began to scream "'the stars were falling down.' She must have thought the world was coming to an end." In Kansas the dust blew for twelve days in a row. Trains and cars stopped running, children didn't go to school, people just huddled inside their homes and waited for it to pass. Viola Cooper recalls:

> We used to get quite a few blizzards after the big one, although I don't remember any as bad as that one. When they hit, all we could do was lie in bed or sit in a chair. You couldn't hardly see across the room even when all the lights was on or lamps were lit. And dust got into everything and on everyone. My mother used to complain about how us kids always had dirty faces. Well now everybody's face was dirty. Dirt was everywhere. We had dirt in our eyes, in our mouths, between our teeth, down our clothes. You'd put wet rags, blankets, sheets, dish towels around the windows and doors to keep the dirt out, but it found some way to come in anyhow no matter how tight you shut things. You'd think it just seeped through the walls.

I had some little pet chickens and I kept them in the house. They'd be just like little dust balls running around, little brown balls of dust. But the cattle and all—it was just pitiful. They'd get the dust in their eyes and lungs and they'd go blind and suffocate. You had to hear the poor creatures moaning and dying. Wild animals too. Millions of them must have died in the blizzards. People died. They'd breathe the dust and die of the dust pneumonia. They'd cough up big gobs of dust and die. Old folks. Little babies died. It just broke your heart to see it.

Some communities had over a thousand hours of storms a year, day after day, some lasting almost two weeks. In 1935 in Guymon, Oklahoma, there were 550 hours of daylight turned into night by

A casualty of the dust storms. Many cattle choked to death from having too much dust in their lungs.

the dust. In Amarillo, Texas, 908 hours. By the end of 1935 the rich plains area—once the wheat belt of America—was a vast desert with shifting sand dunes everywhere. Not only the land, but houses and barns were buried over with dirt. It was the greatest catastrophe that had ever happened to the land in America, and it devastated the lives of millions of the people who lived through it. They tried to hold on as best they could. "We really love the land and we would have tried to stay with it," Viola Cooper recalls.

> We worked hard, trying to keep the farm. In those days, farms didn't have many of the conveniences you have today. Many didn't have electricity or indoor toilets, telephones or plumbing. We got our water from a well. But we loved it. The whole family worked hard trying to keep our heads above water, getting up early to plant and raise wheat, milk the cows and feed the chickens. When the rains stopped coming, we just tried to hang on the best we could. We looked a lot of the time to see if a cloud was coming like Elijah in the days of old, you know in Bible times. We used to meet with neighbors and pray for rain. We used to take our umbrellas along to a meeting just as a joke, but we said you never know, maybe the Lord will answer our prayers. He eventually did but not right then.
>
> By 1935, we knew we were going to lose the farm. We tried every way we could to make money just to hold on, but we were caught between the dust and the depression. I would sell eggs to the local grocery store—they was paying about a nickel a dozen then—or trade them for some beef or bacon which was about a dime a pound. But we couldn't pay our interest and taxes. We had an old truck and they took it away from us because we couldn't make the payments. So we finally got 60 dollars together and we had an old 1928 Chevrolet—and we built a two-wheel trailer and

A farm family prays for rain in the Midwest.

> put all our belongings in it and we went to California where we heard there was work.

In the 1930s nearly four million farmers and their families left the land. Most of them had tried to hang on, but they were overwhelmed by debt and could no longer meet their mortgage payments. Banks and finance companies foreclosed, throwing people off their farms and selling the farms for whatever they could get. Between 1930 and 1935, 750,000 farms were sold.

Sometimes a community of farmers revolted against evictions. One farmer told a reporter:

> If they come to take my farm, I'm going to fight. I'd rather be killed outright than die by starvation. But before I die, I'm going to set fire to my crops, I'm going to burn my house, poison my cattle.

In some places farmers rallied to protect themselves and their neighbors. When a farm was seized and sold at auction, hundreds and sometimes thousands of neighbors would attend and make sure that no outsider bought the farm. They would watch with shotguns under their arms. When the bidding started they would only offer a few dollars for the farmer's possessions and threaten anyone who bid against them. Then everything would be returned to the man who had almost lost it. The following is a description of one such sale from the *Nation* magazine in March 1933:

> The auctioneer mounts the wagon. The first thing offered is a mare. . . . What is he offered, what is he offered, do I hear a bid? He tries to make it sound like an ordinary sale. But the crowd stands silent, grim. At last someone speaks out. Two dollars! Unheard of, unbelievable, why she's worth more than twenty times that!
>
> The farmer holding the mare stands with his head hanging. At last, without raising his eyes he says "Fifteen dollars." ". . . do I hear twenty, twenty? Why she's worth twice as much as that." The auctioneer is still going through the make-believe. He keeps it up for five more minutes. A voice speaks out. "Sell her!" It is not loud but there is insistence in it, like the slice of a plow. . . . The auctioneer hesitates, gives in. "Sold!" After that there is less make-believe. Three more horses are offered. They are knocked down to the farmer with no other bids, for ten dollars, eight dollars, a dollar and a half. The farmer is learning. The machinery comes next. A hayrack, a wagon, two plows, mower, disc-harrow

All over the Midwest, farmers' possessions were seized when they couldn't pay their mortgages and sold to pay their debts.

> pulverizer. A dollar, fifty cents, fifty cents, a quarter, a half a dollar. Sold to the farmer. His means of livelihood are saved to him.

Farmers also challenged sheriffs when they came to enforce a foreclosure and at times drove them away with bullets. One farmer warned potential bidders "anyone buying a place won't find life worth living. Won't no one buy from him, sell to him—there won't be nobody speak to him." And in one case, when a local judge kept foreclosing farms, local farmers became so enraged that they burst into his office one day, yanked him out of his chair, put a rope around his neck, and threatened to hang him from the nearest tree. The judge resigned shortly after that for "reasons of health."

But many families just quit. One day, they just packed their belongings and walked out of their houses, abandoning them forever. Four hundred thousand of them went to California. They took what little savings they had, piled everything and everyone they could in the family jalopy, and took off for the West Coast, where they heard that the crops were good, work was plentiful, and living was easy.

Highway 66 was then the main migrant route that led from the rain-starved fields of the plains states to the lush golden lands of California. But getting there often meant a journey that could be as dangerous as that of ancient sailors voyaging on unknown seas. Many of the cars and trucks were not able to take the punishment of a long trip. They were old and in need of repair. They had to climb over the Rocky Mountains and push their way through the burning deserts of Nevada and California. Many of these ancient cars could climb mountains at speeds of only fifteen to twenty miles an hour, shaking and rattling as they went. If a car broke down, people would be stuck on the side of the road, without money, friends, or family to help. Thus, they listened to the beat of the car's engine as attentively as to a church sermon. A strange noise could send terror into the hearts of a family. They would ask each other, "Is that the bearings? What if a gasket blows? Oil pressure's mighty low. Could there be a crack in the block?" If a family was lucky, the worst that would happen would be a blown tire or a snapped fan belt. Tires could be patched and a piece of rope could replace a fan belt. Sometimes, people simply ran out of gas and money and had to abandon their cars. But all too often, the old jalopy just gave out. Too many people to carry, too many miles to travel. After a while the bodies of dead and dying wrecks of cars lay stretched out alongside the road, pointing toward the goal they had struggled to reach and failed.

What was it like on the road? "We had a tent," recalled Eva Marples, who was ten years old when she and her family made the trip.

> In those days, there weren't many motels and you had to have money to stay in them, which we didn't have. So at night, we would unpack everything by the side of the road, set up the tent and cook in it. It was hard for our folks, but us kids loved it. It was a big adventure. No matter how hard parents were suffering, they always took care of us children first. If parents slept on the ground, the children slept in the car. When there was little food, the children were always fed even if it was no more than fried dough. People begged for water at gas stations. Many attendants wouldn't let you drink unless you was going to buy something.

Ruby Thomas remembered her thirst. She was five years old at the time and as her family was crossing the desert, they ran out of water. "I was so thirsty, I was crying for a drink of water. Dad kept saying wait and I kept crying and finally he said, 'Damn it, shut up!'" Then he stopped the car. He drained some rusty water out of the radiator into a cup and handed it to Ruby's mother, who strained it through a pillowcase and gave it to her to drink.

For some the trip was both too much and too little—too much heat and too much travel, too little food and too little rest. Babies sometimes died and people chipped in to see that they were buried in a marked grave. They felt that since a baby hadn't had much of a life, it should at least have a decent burial. But when old people died, they were sometimes buried in unmarked graves because their families were too poor to pay for a decent funeral. When cars broke down, drivers got spare parts from wherever they could find them and patched the vehicles together. Sometimes people would get stuck in the middle of nowhere and someone would have to walk fifteen or twenty miles to the nearest town to pick up a spare part.

The push was to keep moving. "If only we could get there," they told one another, "things would be all right. In California, there'll be work. In California, there'll be food. In California, we'll buy a house, get a new car, raise a family." They didn't know then that California would not welcome them, would despise them, would call them "Okies" with contempt. They didn't know that California thought them mean and ignorant, criminal and lazy—and would try to keep them out. The only people who had any use for them were the growers who could pay them slave-labor wages—twenty cents an hour and less. This was not enough to keep a family from starving unless the whole family worked together in the fields, father, mother, grandparents, children. And even combined they made barely enough to keep body and soul together. They lived in tents rather than homes, slept on floors rather than beds, wore the same clothes day in and day out, were chased off the land when the job was finished, and had to suffer constant humiliation from others. Eva Marples recalls the insults and the hardships of going to school in California:

> I remember that my teachers used to call me an Okie and criticize me in front of the other children in class. They would criticize my dresses. In those days, girls wore these bloomers under their dresses and mine had so many holes in it that I wouldn't dare go on a swing, 'cause I was afraid the other children would see them and make fun of me. I was always hungry too. Many times, all we had to eat was one can of tomatoes which my mother would fry with flour. For me the biggest treat was when we had an orange—which was usually once a year at Christmas. I used to wonder which of my two brothers I would like my parents to give away so that the rest of us could have more to eat. My daddy couldn't get a job so he invented one. He used to take us children into the foothills around Los Angeles where sheep and cattle grazed and we would gather manure and then go around to people's homes and sell it as fertilizer for their lawns. I think we got fifty cents a sack for it.

Dale Gene Scales remembers that his family was so poor that for a period of time as a young boy, all he had to wear was a bathing suit, and that when he wanted to play baseball, he and his brothers and sisters stuffed cotton into a sock to make a ball and used an ax handle as a bat. (He must have learned something from it because he grew up to play three years of professional baseball for the Chicago White Sox organization.)

One man, who traveled as a child with his father from field to field picking whatever crop was ripe at the time, remembered the rates in the early thirties: "Where we worked, figs paid ten cents a box, grapes or lemons, twenty-five cents an hour, peas paid a penny a pound, lettuce, five cents a crate." The rates differed at different farms, but no matter what the job, most people earned somewhere between $1.00 and $1.50 a day, although there were some who earned as much as $5.00. The larger the family, the more money they could earn. Children often missed school to help in the fields. Even the little income they earned made a difference. They picked cotton until their fingers bled, peas until their backs ached, working a full day in the fields for fifty cents. Dale Gene Scales remembered picking cotton from the third grade until high school.

> As soon as I got home after school let out I would go out in the fields and pick cotton. My mom would make me a peanut butter and jelly sandwich and I would swing my gunny sack over my back and I would go out into the fields until it got dark. And I have never forgotten that even when I was a small child, maybe six or seven years old, sitting down in the field in the dark, looking at my hands all bloody from picking cotton, saying to myself, Dale Gene, this is no way to live. And I vowed I wouldn't be a cotton picker all my life.

Helen Kurch remembers picking grapes and figs in order to save enough money for clothes for school:

> We began to pick grapes at four o'clock in the morning because it would get too hot to work about ten. If I hurried I could make a dollar a day. I didn't mind the grapes as much as the figs. I hate figs till this day. We got ten cents for a hundred-pound bag and you had to crawl on the ground all day. The figs ripened on trees and fell down and I crawled along to pick them up. It was either crawl or stoop and stooping all day can break your back. I worked seven days a week all summer and I made $12 for school clothes.

Many families were defeated by California. Some packed up and went back to Oklahoma, swearing "it was better to starve to death among family and friends than starve among strangers." Others stayed on, but never got beyond working as hired laborers in someone else's field. And others triumphed over adversity. Dale Gene Scales's grit and determination enabled him to become a professional ballplayer, earn a Ph.D., and become a multimillionaire. Others, like Viola Cooper, sustained by their faith in themselves and God, returned to Oklahoma, started to farm over again, and succeeded.

> There's been depressions and other things that people live through though I'd sure hate to go through another one or see my family go through one. But we just don't know what's going to happen in life. We can't throw up our hands and quit though. We just got to keep on keeping on. That's what we did, those of us still living that went through the Dust Bowl days.

CHAPTER FOUR

Work

*O*ne of the ironies of the depression was that while jobs for adults decreased drastically, jobs for children increased.

For almost thirty years, enlightened legislators and socially conscious people agitated for child-labor laws to stop businesses from exploiting children. Although the Supreme Court overturned a congressional law regulating child labor on the grounds that it was unconstitutional for the federal government to interfere with the way companies ran their businesses, many states had passed their own child-labor laws to limit if not prevent the exploitation of children. Progress was being made. In 1900, 25 percent of boys under seventeen and about half as many girls had jobs, most of them full-time. By 1929, only 6 percent of boys and 3 percent of girls were working. The depression then reversed that trend.

With the economic collapse of the country, thousands of farms and factories and many small businesses immediately began to look for a cheap work force that was docile, would work for the lowest possible wages, and would put in long hours without outwardly complaining. They sought children. They were able to exploit them without interference because almost 80 percent of child labor in America in the 1930s was unregulated by the states. Many children worked in family businesses such as farms or in small shops and factories, which were seldom investigated by inspectors. Some states did not even have laws protecting children. As a result, children worked long and grueling hours in textile mills, clothing factories, shoe and leather goods companies, canneries, mines, box plants, and agricultural fields. By 1935, over two million children, nearly 20 percent of the youth population, were working. The number of children working by age was as follows:

Under 10 years of age	10,000–20,000
Between 10–13	250,000
Between 14–15	400,000
Between 16–17	1,500,000

Many farm families were tenant farmers or sharecroppers. They did not own the land they worked. They were obligated to a landlord, who expected the farmer to produce a maximum amount of crops and to use any and all members of his family to work in the fields. Children as young as six or seven worked alongside their parents and sometimes their grandparents and great-grandparents.

One of the most brutal farm jobs for children during the depression was picking cotton. In the South particularly, most cotton was picked by black laborers and white tenant farmers. The system was designed to bring profit to the man who owned the land while keeping the farmer in debt throughout his life. The farmer was only entitled to a share of the crop and out of his share he had to pay for his rent, supplies, tools, and whatever food and clothing he bought at the company store. Thus, the tenant farmer needed his children to help him produce enough to pay his debts. Nothing caused greater fear for a farmer than to hear his landlord say that one of the farmer's

During the depression, many children had to work to help support their families. This girl picked strawberries in California.

children was of "no account and couldn't hold up his end." This meant that the landlord might kick him and his family off the land.

The working day was from "can see to can't see," that is, from daylight to dark. The children and the rest of the family would begin to pick as early as possible in the morning because it was the coolest part of the day. In the South, temperatures often reached over one hundred degrees in the summertime.

Pickers carried a long white bag slung over their right shoulders and trailing along the ground. Using both hands, they picked the cotton balls from the plant, trying to avoid being cut by the sharp leaves that surrounded it, a feat impossible to do for any length of time. As a result, the pickers' hands were cut, tired, cramped, and aching by the time picking was over.

Because cotton was picked in the middle of summer, the heat was intense. A cotton bag held up to 400 pounds. An experienced ten-year-old child could pick about 150 pounds in a day. As the bag filled up, it became heavier and heavier and had to be dragged farther and farther as the sun continued to beat down. Since cotton grows close to the ground, the pickers had to bend down, stoop, or crawl to pick it.

Chopping or weeding cotton was another grueling job for children who worked in the fields. A child used a heavy hoe to chop out the weeds that sprung up around the cotton. Many southern children buried their childhood in those cotton fields.

For all their hard labor, tenant farmer children were never paid. They worked only to pay off their family's debts. Some may have

This child worked in the tomato vineyards in New Jersey.

attended school briefly when the cotton season was over, but an education rarely led to a life beyond the fields. Most children of tenant farmers were doomed to follow in their parents' footsteps. Landlords and the white community in general did not encourage black children to go beyond the fifth grade. One racist landlord expressed the general feeling of whites in the South when he noted, "When a nigger goes to school beyond the fifth grade, he tends to get uppity and you have to teach him his place."

Another farm job employing many children was picking tobacco leaves. When tobacco plants are ready for picking they can be eight feet high. Since all the leaves from top to bottom must be picked, children who picked started with bottom leaves, crawling on the ground or bending over to do so. Then they had to reach as high as they could to get the upper leaves. If a leaf broke they could lose their job, for a broken leaf was unusable.

The biggest industrial employer of children was the textile mills. Children started to work at the age of ten and sometimes younger to help support their families. While children working at machines could eventually do almost as much work as an adult, they would receive one-third to one-quarter of the pay, from three to six dollars a week for a fifty- to sixty-hour week.

For many children just starting out in textile mills, the job could be terrifying. The factory room was filled with machines all whirring, banging, and clattering. These machines had gears and teeth that could easily crush or rip flesh. One fourteen-year-old girl recounted her fear on her first day at work:

> As I stood looking at all the different wheels turning this way and that, it looked like a jig saw to me. I was scared to death watching girls place their hands on different parts of the machines which are in motion from 7 to 5. The machines frightened me so much that the girl who was teaching me told the

In the South, it had long been a custom for the children of the poor to work in the mills, even before the depression. Some were paid as little as two dollars for a sixty-hour week.

> foreman I was too young to do the work and too small a child to be put on these machines.

Another young girl told a college student the story of her life in the factory, which began when she was fourteen years old. She said she was a sickly child and was advised by a doctor not to work. But the depression forced her into the mills; and because, like many children, she had no skills, she wound up with the most monotonous and poorest-paid job in the factory:

> This is my daily program.
>
> At 5:30 it is time for me to get up. I am tired and sleepy. After I get up, I hurriedly eat my breakfast and I am ready to go

to work. It is a chilly winter morning but I know it will be hot in the mill. I start on my three-mile walk to the factory. As I walk, I see others hurrying to work. I look at the older people and I wonder if they feel the resentment every morning as I do or if as the years go by, their spirits are deadened.

I arrive at the factory. The sight that I dread to see meets my eyes; the line of unemployed people waiting for the boss to come and hoping for work.

As I open the door, a force of hot stuffy air greets me. I rush to the machine as all the girls do, to get ready so that when the whistle blows, we can start working. When doing piece work, every minute counts.

I seam men's heavy underwear. After I finish twelve union suits, I get a check for .06 for size fifty and 4½ cents for smaller sizes. At the end of the week, I paste my checks in a book and give my book to the boss, who pays according to the number of checks that I have. After finishing a dozen union suits, I tie them up and carry them to the bin. The dozens are heavy and grow heavier as the day goes on. The day goes on and I throw my dozen up on the top and it very often comes down on me. Of course, I fall. . . .

After my many trips to the bin for my work, and my finishing each dozen, tying it up, signing my number on the check, then carrying it to the next bin, I am so tired that my body and mind go numb. The toilet does not flush very well, but it never does anyway. When I come to the water fountain, no matter how tired and numb I feel, I am always angry and disgusted. The water is lukewarm. The fountain is rusty and filthy. But my trip to the fountain is a stimulant because I am always glad to get back to my bench.

A girl of 18 came to the mill from high school. This girl is not used to hard work, standing on her legs. Now she walks with a cane. The city doctor cannot cure her. Now she leads the life of a recluse, alone, bitter, hating life. Only last year she was a healthy, eager child, loving life and having wonderful plans for the future.

As usual, half my lunch has been spoiled. I can either put it on the table where I keep my work and where it becomes squashed, or I can put it in a box under my bench and give the rats the first choice.

After a monotonous afternoon, it is almost time to go home. We have three minutes to put our coats on; then we wait in our respective aisles. All eyes are on the boss, waiting for the signal. Then we rush out. As I walk home, I can see some of the people for whom my class works. The priest rolls by in his car. The superintendent's daughter waits for her father in his car. I think of my father who has to stay one more hour in the mill, then trudge home where his daughter is too tired to greet him.

Young women had an especially difficult time finding work. There were relatively few jobs for women outside of the factories, mostly domestic services, secretarial work, teaching, and service industries. Often male bosses would offer a young girl a job if she was attractive and willing to exchange sex for work. Even when there were legitimate job offers, women had to endure many hardships to get them. And most jobs meant long hours for little pay. Molly, a seventeen-year-old girl, reported to a college student who interviewed her:

I had to plug away at this ever since I left school two years ago. Not even much time to dream about school days now. First I had a domestic job, paid me $2.00 a week. Eighty-three hours of that! I made $3.00 a week on the next one but I had to grind out 93 hours to earn it. I've been house servanting now. Only work 45 hours and I salt down $2.00 a week. But the work frankly

> stinks. I'd do anything to get away. . . . I'd sure like to work in a department store. Yeah. Right behind the counter. Make me feel like a fancy lady just handling them pretty clothes.

Kate Templeton quit school at the age of fourteen to help out at home. She walked four hours a day to and from her job in a shoe factory. There was public transportation but it was more important to save money.

> You did everything to save a penny. Pennies mattered because they were worth something. You could buy 3 donuts for a dime and a loaf of stale bread for three and a half cents, coffee for a nickel, and a large can of salmon for a quarter.

To survive, some parents brought work home for the entire family. While this was a common practice during the late nineteenth and early twentieth centuries, it had died out by the late 1920s. With the depression it returned. One family strung safety pins on a wire and collectively worked a total of 150 hours a week, yet could earn no more than three to four dollars.

Mary, who grew up in Newark, New Jersey, remembered that when she was eight, she made dolls' dresses from the time she got home from school.

> I got home at 3:30 and sat down and worked at the kitchen table till 5:00 making dolls' dresses. We tried to do other things, like sew men's clothes or make powder puffs. But the clothes were too heavy for my eleven-year-old brother to carry from the factory. The powder puffs made me sick for some reason. So it was dolls' dresses.
>
> We had dinner at 5:00 and afterwards I worked from six to nine when it was time to go to bed. My two brothers worked

> alongside of me. Even my little four-year-old brother Jack helped when he could.
>
> My job was cutting the threads. There were other steps to making dresses but my job was cutting threads. I did this every day for years. It didn't matter if it was raining or the sun was shining, light or dark out. We had to work long hours because the pay was so little. I thought I would go crazy, the work was so tedious.

Mary at least had the advantage of going to school in the hope that one day she would have a better life. Many parents felt so defeated that they kept their children out of school so they could work. One mother said,

> It's better to go to work and bring money home. Schools are only for the rich. Poor people must work for their living. School does poor people no good. All my seven children went to work at 14. The poor have to work to clothe and feed themselves.

Many children under the age of ten worked at a variety of street jobs such as shining shoes or delivering and selling newspapers. Some newsboys were as young as six. Newsboys often sold newspapers after school, sometimes from four to midnight and even later. The system was cruel and one-sided. Not only did newsboys have to sell and deliver papers, they also had to collect money from subscribers on their route. If the subscriber failed to pay, the money was taken out of the newsboy's wages. Nor could the newsboy cancel the subscription of a nonpayer without permission of the newspaper. If the newsboy worked in the rain and a paper got wet, he had to pay for it. As a result, a newsboy's average wage was about four and a half cents an hour.

During the depression exploitation of children was the rule. Children in one factory earned fifty-three cents for a week of their labor. Some factories paid three to eight cents an hour for child labor, depending on the age of the child. The average wage for a child was about $2.50 a week. For children to earn $5.00 to $8.00 often meant that they had to work twelve hours a day, six days a week. When a boss was fined $100 by a state inspector in Pennsylvania for allowing hazardous working conditions in his factory, he docked thirty-three cents from the pay of each child to make up the fine.

Yet a child considered himself lucky if he had a steady job. One fourteen-year-old boy, who was the sole support of his mother and nine brothers and sisters, related his desperate search to find work:

> I heard about a job at a clothing store. So they put me on as a general helper. I learned nothing and it only lasted a month. I looked in the newspapers and went by factories for a month until I got a job cleaning hats. But business was slack so I was laid off again. I got a swell job as a messenger for a telegraph company but things was rotten and after a year, I got laid off again. I got another job in a shoe factory where we worked very hard and the wages was low. But that didn't last too long.

Another teenager kept a record of his employment and unemployment:

Job in factory	2 months
Unemployed	4 weeks
Wrapper in shoe factory	1 month
Unemployed	6 weeks
Sewer in clothing factory	3 months
Unemployed	1 month
Another clothing factory	3 weeks
Unemployed	1 year

Not only were the hours long and the pay little, but working conditions were usually terrible. Many factories were filthy, with toilets that didn't work and impure drinking water. They were infested with rats, mice, and bugs. In one agricultural camp, thirteen young boys lived in a room that was sixteen feet by sixteen feet and had only nine single beds. The room had no toilets or washing facilities.

There were many accidents and deaths. Most children were more terrified of being fired than of being injured and often agreed to do dangerous work rather than lose their jobs. One fifteen-year-old boy fell off a scaffold working on a building and broke his arms and legs. A twelve-year-old newsboy got too close to an unguarded printing press and was dragged between wheels that crushed his arm and foot. Inexperienced boys lost fingers in sawmills when their hands got too close to the saw. A young girl lost four fingers from one hand in a machine at a textile mill. A truck loaded with children working on a tobacco farm overturned on a road, seriously injuring many and trapping three children underneath the truck. Their friends tried to free them, but the truck was too heavy to lift. It caught fire and the children were burned to death.

While most children and adults accepted these working conditions in the early years of the depression out of necessity, there was growing resentment and rebellion among all workers. Mary spoke for millions of workers when she cried out:

> There is a terrible rage in my heart. I want to learn what crushes out the lives of workers and what takes the children of these people and places them in stuffy factories, even before they have time to fill their lungs with fresh air.

In the late thirties her question would be answered.

CHAPTER FIVE

Organizing

When fourteen-year-old Anne Timpson (then Anne Burlak) decided to struggle for the rights of working people to earn a decent living, most of America's workers were in a desperate condition. By 1930, millions of people were working ten or twelve hours a day, six days a week. Working families often made so little money that they were forced to live in slums. Often they had to buy their food at high prices in stores that were owned by the company for which they worked. In those times, any family whose income was more than seventy dollars a month considered itself lucky. Most families had to go into debt each week because they couldn't earn enough to meet expenses. One family's budget was like this:

Rent	$25 a month
Gas/electric	$10
Food	$35
Transportation	$3
Clothes	$2
Total	$75
Income	–$70
Debt each month	$5

Sometimes only a gallows sense of humor enabled workers to survive. At Biggs Manufacturing Company in Detroit the pay was so bad—men were paid ten cents an hour and women four cents—that the standard joke among the employees was, "If poison doesn't work, try Biggs."

Many jobs were marginal. Out of the 48 million people employed in 1930, only 5 million worked in heavy industries such as iron, steel, coal, and automobiles; 13 million more were in the professions or management. The remaining 30 million worked at a variety of jobs. There were 1,654,000 domestic workers, 1,000,000 secretaries, 292,000 cooks, 310,000 janitors, 28,000 bakers, and 249,000 telephone operators, as well as an indeterminate number of fruit and vegetable pickers, carnival workers, window cleaners, rag stuffers, and migrant workers. Most of them were forced to work longer hours for less pay and did so without complaint for fear that they would lose the jobs they had. One woman wrote to the president of the United States:

> When my poor husband gets home he is too weary to eat. Two weeks ago he worked thirty hours without stopping only to gulp a few bites and came home at 2 o'clock, bathed and went to bed and at seven that evening they wanted him to go back and they never paid him a dime in overtime.

Anne Timpson recalled the lack of job security workers had in those days:

> If a worker lost his or her job, there was no unemployment insurance. If they were too old to work, there was no social security. If they or any of their family became ill, there was no medical assistance. If they couldn't pay the rent, they were evicted from their homes, their belongings dumped on the sidewalk and the family left to get along as best it could. The only thing between them

and starvation was relief or charity, and there was never enough of that to go around. Some people became so depressed they committed suicide.

During this period, workers had no rights. They were not permitted to join or organize a union or even complain about working conditions, which were often dirty and dangerous. Many companies had their own private police force and a network of company spies. A worker could be fired for any reason or no reason at all. Anyone who protested or tried to organize a union might be beaten up as well as fired and blacklisted from working anywhere else. In some parts of the country, union organizers were murdered.

Strikes often turned violent during the depression. Companies hired local police and private gunmen to intimidate, beat, and even kill workers striking for the right to organize, for better working conditions, and for higher wages.

For almost a hundred years, American labor leaders had tried to change this system, sometimes with violent strikes, sometimes with political pressure, sometimes with quiet organizing. Progress was slow and limited. Very few companies kept workers to an eight-hour day or recognized unions. By the time of the Great Depression, most workers were still unorganized. And many of the unions were reluctant to strike or to challenge the owners in any significant way. This would radically change by the end of the depression.

For most Americans, the depression came as a shock. They were caught by surprise and unable to understand what had happened and why. But for a small group of people, the depression had been long expected and was even welcomed. They were the radicals—the Socialists and Communists—who for eighty years had been waiting for Karl Marx's prediction of the collapse of capitalism to come true. To them, the Great Depression marked the end of the old world of capitalism and the beginning of a new one in which the workers would triumph.

Anne Timpson was one of the radicals who was determined to change the capitalistic world. Her father had fled Russia during the revolution against the czar in 1905 and emigrated to America, where he found a job in a steel mill. A few years before the beginning of the depression, Anne dreamed of becoming a schoolteacher, but she found that she had to help support her family. At the age of fourteen she went to work in a silk mill, where there was a small but weak union.

"I became very interested in unions then," she says, "because I was being paid $9.00 for a 54-hour week while young men who were doing the same job were being paid $14.00. When I complained about it, I was told, 'Well, girls don't need as much money as boys do.'" When she tried to join the union, she was turned down—because she was a teenager and a woman. But this rejection only made her more enthusiastic for unions and increased her desire to join. She attended union demonstrations and was sometimes arrested, but because she was then only sixteen, she was released. Finally, in 1929, just before the stock market crash, she joined the National Textile Workers Union. Despite her youth, the union leaders were so impressed with her spirit and courage that they gave her one of the most dangerous assignments for a union organizer. The union sent her to the South to help organize the textile mills. Her salary, when it was paid, was ten dollars a week.

The working conditions in the textile mills of the South were among the worst in America. Men, women, and children worked ten to twelve hours a day in these hot, dirty, dangerous conditions for as little as four dollars a week. There were no unions in the mills, and organizers who were brave enough to try and organize one were beaten or killed.

Anne was sent to organize a mill in Greenville, South Carolina. "The union thought that my being a young girl would protect me against violence. None of us knew the South too well and that my age would make no difference."

When she arrived at Greenville, Anne began to organize very cautiously. She would visit a mill late at night to talk to workers on the midnight shift, when there were no guards around. As the workers ate their dinner in the fields outside the mill, Anne sat with them in the dark talking to them about organizing. During the day, she visited them secretly in their homes.

> There was a custom in the South of prayer meetings being held in private homes on Sunday mornings. We took advantage of this. We would visit a home on Sunday, not for prayer, but to have a union meeting. The owner's son or daughter would sit outside to warn us if the deputy sheriffs were around. If they signaled us they were coming, we'd suddenly stop our union business, take out our hymn books and sing a hymn like "Nearer My God to

> Thee," as if we were having a prayer meeting. Then, when it was safe, we'd go back to organizing.

Late one afternoon Anne was addressing a group of workers at a mill and passing out leaflets. Suddenly a caravan of cars drove up with about thirty people in them and surrounded her.

> Whenever I tried to speak, they began blowing their car horns and heckling me so I couldn't be heard. Some young boys had long switches and they tried to hit me in the legs. I wondered why they didn't try to rush me, but it was still daylight and I guess there were too many people around. I felt I should try to get back to town before dark. As I started walking back, they got into their cars and began to follow behind me. I was sure they were waiting until it was dark. All of a sudden, I saw a taxicab on the street and the driver looked familiar. I remembered he had given me a lift two weeks earlier when I was hitchhiking and he had been friendly. I jumped into his cab and he recognized me and asked what was going on. I said, "There's no time to explain. There's a mob after me. Will you help?" He said, "Sure," and we took off. The mob followed us. I told the driver why they were after me and that I was afraid he might turn me over to them. He told me not to worry. I asked what if they catch us and overpower you. "Maybe," he said, "but first they got to catch us and secondly, I got my gun in the glove compartment and I'll use it if I have to." He turned his headlights off and began to drive in the dark at high speed. The other cars pursued us and we drove wildly around back country roads until he came to a house he knew and pulled his car behind it so that he was hidden from the road. The other cars drove right by us. The taxi driver then took me to a safe place and friends came and got me. They sent in another organizer to replace me. Two weeks after the new organizer

> arrived, she was kidnapped by a mob in Greenville, taken out into the woods, and severely beaten. I'm sure it wasn't meant for her. I'm sure it was meant for me.

The attempt to organize the Greenville mills failed. The depression made it harder to organize workers because people were terrified about losing their jobs. But if workers were too cautious to demonstrate, Anne Timpson found that the unemployed did not have the same concern.

> Because it was so hard to organize workers in the beginning of the Depression, we first organized the unemployed. Sixteen million people were out of work and many of them felt they had nothing to lose. So we began to campaign for unemployment insurance, for relief, for the government to provide jobs. We organized hunger marches on Washington. We would start out in New England with about a hundred workers and begin to march to the White House and Congress. Along the way, people would join us and the hundreds would soon be thousands. Everywhere we went, we would stop and explain to the people who we were and why we were marching. We didn't talk about socialism then. The American people weren't ready for it. But we talked to them about getting help for the unemployed. At one meeting in Maryland, the police tried to break through our lines because black and white people were marching together and it was against the law to do so. They couldn't break through so they began beating people and Ben Gold who was the leader of the march came out to see what was going on and he was immediately hit with one of the clubs and knocked down. Then a group of four policeman stood around and clubbed him as he lay on the ground. One of the young men in our group became angry and threw a soda pop bottle and hit one of the policeman on the side

> of the head. This policeman straightened up, drew out his gun and said, "I'm going to shoot one of you dirty so and sos." And he started walking up toward us with his gun drawn and I thought to myself, if he starts shooting, every policeman will start shooting. Maybe if I go towards him, being a young girl, he won't shoot me. So I walked towards him and I said in a calm voice, "Put that gun away. No one here is armed, put it away, you're going to hurt someone." And when I got within six feet of him, he put his gun away. And I have a feeling that we avoided a real massacre that day.

Organizing demonstrations was only part of Anne Timpson's work. She was a member of the Unemployed Councils, organizations formed by the Socialist and Communist parties, which fought for the rights of the unemployed, peacefully if possible, militantly if necessary. The councils led demonstrations on city governments for relief and jobs. Perhaps their most popular and effective tactic was to stop evictions.

> When people were evicted from their homes, someone would come and get us and say, "Mr. and Mrs. Smith at such and such an address were being evicted." We would immediately run down there and organize the neighbors and take the furniture that the landlord's men were carrying out of the house and carry it back in. And we would prevent the eviction from taking place with our bodies. And most of the time the police would just stand by and do nothing because they were outnumbered and also because many of them didn't like evicting people. After we put the furniture back, we would mount a guard around the house and prevent the landlord from getting in. After awhile, most city governments declared a moratorium on evictions. But they wouldn't have done so if the people themselves hadn't taken action.

But the real battle for workers' rights was to be fought in the mills and factories of America. As the depression dragged on, factory owners took advantage of the crisis to squeeze the most out of their employees. They felt that the workers would be so afraid of losing their jobs that they would not protest when hours were increased and wages reduced. Many workers wrote to President Roosevelt or his secretary of labor, Frances Perkins, to complain.

> Dear Miss Perkins,
> We work in a Woolstock concern. We handle discarded rags. We work ten hours a day for six days. In the grime and dirt of a nation. We go home tired and sick—dirty and disgusted. . . average wage 16 dollars. We handle diseased rags all day. Tuberculosis roaming loose, unsanitary conditions . . . slaves, slaves of the depression. I am young . . . a high school education—no recreation, no fun—Pardon, ma'am, I want to live! Do you deny me that right? As an American citizen I ask you—what must we do?

The answer was—strike! Eventually the fear of losing a job gave way to the anger of being exploited. The radical organizers like Anne Timpson continued to agitate for labor reforms and decent working conditions. Their message was heard throughout the country. Workers began to recognize that the only way to secure their rights to decent wages and working conditions and reasonable hours was to fight for them. In 1933–1934, a series of strikes broke out all over America. Some of them turned into open warfare. The factory owners met the strikes with armed guards, spies, "goon squads," and, at times, bullets. The casualty lists of dead and dying workers were high. Hundreds were beaten, maimed, and killed. Tens of thousands lost their jobs. The strikers occasionally met violence with violence, but their strength was not in weapons but in determination. They marched, they picketed, they sat down inside facto-

Even in the South, where strikes were relatively rare, workers fought for the right to organize. Often, women led the protests.

ries and refused to move. In 1934, strikes led by labor radicals won victories at the Electric Auto-Lite plant in Toledo, Ohio; in the trucking industry in Minneapolis, Minnesota; and on the docks in San Francisco. Under growing union pressure, the federal government passed legislation that supported the workers' right to organize and provided Social Security benefits for older workers who had retired. Major victories were won in the auto and steel industries in the late 1930s, sometimes smoothly, sometimes with much bloodshed. By the time World War II began, the American labor movement had triumphed. Unions had won the right to represent the workers and to bargain with the owners for decent wages and working conditions. To Anne Timpson, although the victory wasn't complete, it represented a major triumph.

Unemployed workers, demonstrating for jobs and government aid, were often arrested and beaten. Black protesters were usually treated more harshly by police than white protesters were.

I think the labor movement gave a real purpose to my life. Not the kind of purpose that some Americans have about making a lot of money and being a success and not be concerned about anybody else. I learned as a teenager that being a working class woman I could not improve my life without improving the lives of my class. I could not stop the attacks on myself without stopping the attacks on the working class as a whole. In spite of all the attacks and all the persecution I saw around me, and the vicious ways in which workers were being treated, I was confident that eventually we were going to win—and we did!

CHAPTER SIX

Blacks in the Depression

An elderly black man recalls growing up in the depression:

> The Negro was born in depression so the Great American Depression didn't mean too much to him. The best he could be was a porter or shoe shine boy. It only became official when it happened to the white man.

For black people in America during the 1930s, economic depression was a fact of life. Unemployment was always high in the black community; economic opportunities were always limited. The discrimination against black people was profound and widespread throughout the United States. Few stores and factories would hire black workers. Few unions would accept them as members. The few companies that hired blacks usually employed them in the most menial jobs. In the southern states, blacks were segregated from whites. They attended separate schools, sat in separate sections on buses and in movie theaters, used separate drinking fountains and separate rest rooms in public places, and worshiped in separate churches. Black people were not allowed to vote or serve on juries, or to become peace officers, judges, or government officials. Lynchings were so common in the South that newspapers didn't even bother to report many of them. Black people were denied their rights by the courts and by both federal and state legislatures. In the North, although segregation was not official, there were unwritten laws that prevented blacks from entering many private and public places. Still, there was more freedom of movement for black people in the North and they were not subjected to the vicious oppression as in the South. They could vote and attend schools and ride on buses and sit where they wanted. Yet, the prejudice against them was as deep as it was in the South. Race riots, when they occurred, occurred in the North.

As bad as things were before the depression, the crash only made things worse. From the end of the Civil War until 1929, there were many jobs that white Americans considered unsuitable for themselves. This racist attitude resulted in the employment of large numbers of black people as janitors, barbers, elevator operators, street cleaners, garbage collectors, waiters and hotel employees, porters on trains, maids, cooks, laborers, and shoe shine men. On occasion, black workers found jobs as cowboys or railroad firemen, or worked in a few industrial plants such as slaughterhouses and steel mills. A privileged few were able to make a living as entertainers. When the depression came, suddenly these jobs were eagerly sought after by unemployed whites who would grab any job they could get. Not only did they compete with blacks for the same jobs, but many times they completely shut them out. In some places whites would beat or kill any black person who tried to keep his job. The worse the depression became, the more whites demanded those jobs that had traditionally belonged to blacks. In 1930, the year after the crash, unemployment among black workers was 15.7 percent compared to 9 percent for whites. In 1931, 35 percent of blacks were unemployed

A typical Harlem street scene in the 1930s. Despite the fact that the depression hurt black workers more than white, there was a strong community feeling among most black people.

and 24 percent of whites. The following year 56 percent of the black community was out of work compared to 39 percent of the white.

Anna Arnold Hedgemen describes what Harlem was like when she was growing up in her autobiography, *The Trumpet Sounds:*

> The crashing drop of wages drove Negroes back to the already crowded hovels east of Lenox Avenue. In many blocks, one toilet served a floor of four apartments. Most of the apartments had no private bathrooms or even the luxury of a public bath. All of these tenements were filthy and vermin ridden.
>
> Many families had been reduced to living below street level. Packed in damp, rat-ridden dungeons, they existed in squalor

not too different from Arkansas sharecroppers. . . . There were only slits for a window and a tin can for a toilet. . . . Compared to the 20 to 25 percent of their income white families paid for rent, Negro tenants paid 40 to 45 percent. More than half the Negro families were forced to take in lodgers. Frequently all members of a family slept together in one room. Envied was the family who had a night worker as a lodger for he would occupy a bed for the day that would be rented out at night. If a family had a bathtub, it too would be covered with boards and rented out [as a bed].

. . . a large mass of Negroes were faced with the realities of starvation and turned to public relief . . . [but] the Home Relief

When times got really hard, some people could stay alive only through relief. Families brought their own plates for food and often had to wait on lines for hours.

Bureau only allowed eight cents a day for food. Meanwhile men, women and children combed the streets and searched garbage cans for food, foraging with dogs and cats. . . .

Richard Wright, in his autobiographical novel, *Black Boy,* writes about what it was like for a black youth growing up in the depression years to have a job a white man felt did not belong to a black man. Wright took a job as a janitor in an optical company in order to learn how to make eyeglasses and earn a decent living. One day, he asked two white employees named Reynolds and Pease, who seemed friendly, to teach him the trade.

"What are you trying to do, get smart, nigger?" Reynolds asked me.

"No sir," I said.

I was baffled. Perhaps he just did not want to help me. I went to Pease to remind him that the boss said that I was to be given a chance to learn the trade.

"Nigger, you think you're white, don't you?"

"No sir."

"You're acting mighty like it."

"I'm only doing what the boss told me to do," I said.

Pease shook his fist in my face.

"This is a *white* man's work around here," he said.

Eventually Richard Wright was forced to quit.

When threats failed to make a black man quit a job, violence was used. As one reporter noted, in the South "dead men not only tell no tales, they create vacancies." Frank Kincaid, a black fireman, was working on a train one night when suddenly a shotgun roared out and a load of buckshot caught him in the head and killed him. A few seconds later, his body was dumped on the side of the tracks and a white man took his place and the train pulled out. By 1933, seven black railroad men had been murdered and seven others wounded.

Lynchings and lynch trials of blacks on phony charges also increased in the South during the depression, and being young was no protection. In 1931, seventeen-year-old Clarence Norris and two friends jumped aboard a freight train in Georgia headed for Birmingham, Alabama, and possible work. They were children of black sharecroppers who lived in poverty and for whom the depression was especially hard. A group of white teenagers was also on the train and tried to force the black youths off. A fight broke out and the black teenagers managed to throw the whites off the train. Angry at being humiliated, the whites, none of whom was seriously injured, notified the local sheriff, who telegraphed ahead to stop the train and arrest the black youths. At a little town called Paint Rock, the sheriff, his deputies, and a number of armed white men stopped the train and arbitrarily arrested nine of the twenty black youths aboard. Most of them did not know one another. There were still several whites on the train as well. To everyone's surprise, two of them turned out to be young white women dressed as boys. Clarence Norris recalled what happened that day:

> When we reached this little old town of Paint Rock, Alabama, there was a bunch of white men with rifles and shotguns waiting for us. They took us off the train and some of them was saying, "Let's lynch these 'niggers.' Let's take them to a tree and hang them." And there was two men with uniforms and buttons. I don't know if they was policemen or firemen or what, but they had these brass buttons and they said, "No. Let's take them to jail." And we never did see no white women. The next day, they brought these two white women to the jail—Victoria Price and Ruby Bates. They lined us up and the sheriff says to Victoria, "Which ones had you?" And she pointed out four of us. "This one

> and that one, that one and that one." Then they asked Ruby Bates. But she don't say nothing. Then the sheriff says, "No need to ask her. The others must have had her." And that's how a rape charge was framed against us. I never will forget it. That's the way it happened.

The nine youths—collectively known as "the Scottsboro Boys," named for the town in which they were tried—were convicted of rape and sentenced to death. Seven of the nine were teenagers. The death sentence was imposed despite the fact that one of the so-called victims eventually denied she was raped. In addition, there was no physical evidence that the women had been attacked. Even though the Supreme Court overturned the death convictions, Clarence Norris remained in jail almost twenty years before he finally escaped from an Alabama prison. In 1980, he was pardoned by the state of Alabama.

By the middle of the depression it was estimated that over half the black work force in southern cities was unemployed. In the rural areas, where most of the black population worked on farms, black sharecroppers earned $275 a year compared to $417 for white sharecroppers. Laborers earned an average of $175 a year compared to $232 for whites. Black farmers depended upon cotton, and during the depression, prices fell so low that only a very few were able to make enough money to provide for their families. Many went broke or deeper in debt. Even when a young black person was given a job, he was at the mercy of the whites for whom he worked. Henry Winston, who grew up in Mississippi, remembered working as a caddie at a golf course when he was ten years old.

> There was this one man who used to play every day and we all hated to caddie for him. He had this cruel habit of taking a golf ball in his hand and cracking it against the head of whoever was

> caddying for him. Then he would laugh and say, "I want to see which is harder, a golf ball or a nigger's head." To show there was no hard feelings on his part, he would give me a dime—as if money would make the pain go away. I wanted to throw the money in his face, but my family needed the dime—and I needed the job.

The only thing that enabled many black families to survive was public assistance, and even there they faced bigotry. Before the depression, there was very little relief available to anyone. There were no federal programs and the states had limited funds for public assistance. In the South not only did fewer black people than whites receive government help, but the amount of assistance they received was almost one-third less. In Atlanta, Georgia, the average white relief check was $32.66, while blacks received an average of $19.29. The argument given was that "blacks need less than whites."

Frank "Stretch" Johnson's life was dramatically changed by the Great Depression. He was twelve years old when the crash came.

> When the depression began we were living in poverty like so many other people in our neighborhood. My father was a baseball player. He was of star quality but he could only play in the Negro Leagues at the time and they didn't pay very much. Not enough to support a family. He was a very talented man. He could recite Shakespeare by the yard. He was one of the most talented men in the whole town. He was deeply frustrated that he couldn't support the family. I remember that something everybody did in those days was to throw what they called rent parties. My mother was a great cook and she would cook up a whole batch of food and we would buy some liquor and people would come over and for a small amount of money, they could eat and drink. And we would make enough money to pay the rent for that month. But since everybody was doing it, you couldn't do it too often. So we

Some blacks received work on local, state, or federal projects, like these workers hired to clear a vacant lot.

> had to move a lot. Fortunately during the depression, many landlords were willing to give you the first three months free. So we would move in and after three months, when we wouldn't pay the rent, we'd move out and find another place where we could live for three more months.

Frank remembered his father looking for work whenever there was even the rumor of a job. But for every position that became available, hundreds of men showed up, and it was rare—almost impossible—that a black man would be hired before a white one. The only job that was still open to black people, when it could be found, was domestic work.

Unemployment was much higher among black workers because of discrimination. The rumor of a job could attract hundreds if not thousands of people to apply.

Black women used to go up to the Bronx and stand on a certain street corner and housewives, white housewives, would go out and pick women to work for them—to do a day's work. And we called it the slave market in our community. Because that's what we were essentially—slaves. The big difference between slavery in the thirties and slavery under chattel slavery was that we didn't belong to a particular plantation owner—we belonged to all of them. I remember this one home my grandmother worked in that belonged to a wealthy family. Sometimes, I would meet her there. I remember all the toys and sporting equipment that was on display in the rooms of the kids living there. They had hockey sticks, footballs, football shoulder pads, helmets, ice-skates, base-

> ball gloves, basketballs. I couldn't even afford to buy a pair of basketball shoes. I had to borrow a pair with holes in them to go play basketball.

As the depression settled into the black community, its impact was devastating. Men turned to alcohol; theft increased. Frank's father became caught in this morass.

> Finally, he became so frustrated that he tried to steal a pocketbook. He wasn't a thief so he got caught right away. It wasn't for himself that he did it. It was for us, to put some food on the table. The judge sentenced him to prison for a year. That was the worst moment in all our lives. It devastated our family. We had to split up for a while and go live with relatives. It was the worst moment in my life.

One way out was education. Ever since the end of slavery, the black community had a great faith that education would be the road that would allow their children to escape poverty and racial prejudice. Despite the intense discrimination they suffered, an increasing number of black people had been getting educated. Adult illiteracy in the black community dropped from 45 to 16 percent between 1900 and 1930. In the same period, enrollment doubled in public schools and the number of college students increased from two thousand to fourteen thousand. One of the great tragedies of the depression was that it ended the chances of education for tens of thousands of black teenagers.

> I was one of the brightest students in my high school. In the eighth grade, I scored the highest in a spelling exam for all eighth grade students in the United States. I was on the honor roll frequently. People thought that one day I would be a lawyer, doctor or minister. But to go to college cost $100–$200 dollars a

> year—which was a huge amount of money for us in those days. My family could hardly pay the rent or buy food. College was something very few black people could even dream of. So I quit school to find work. I got a job delivering milk in the morning. I used to get food that way, drinking whatever was left over. I worked as a pinboy in a bowling alley. Eventually, I got a job as an elevator boy in a department store. I was really determined to find work, even if it meant having several jobs at once and working 15 to 16 hours a day. All of it was marginal. None of it had a future. I don't know what would have happened to me if I continued down this path.

Then an event happened that completely changed Frank's life. In 1932, the Cotton Club opened. Run by gangsters, the Cotton Club provided black entertainers for white audiences. No blacks were allowed in the club as patrons, with the exception of celebrities such as Joe Louis, the world heavyweight boxing champion, and Stepin Fetchit, a famous movie character actor who played roles of a stereotyped black man.

Shortly after the Cotton Club opened, Frank's thirteen-year-old sister went for an audition as a dancer and got a job. The family's life began to change for the better. Frank's sister taught him and his younger brother how to dance. Within weeks, they had worked out a dance routine and were hired by the club. They were a big hit. Eventually Frank went on to college and fulfilled his lifelong dream of becoming a college professor.

Despite the hardships and deprivations, life did improve in some areas for America's black community during the depression. As a result of the intense efforts of Eleanor Roosevelt, the president's wife, jobs were made available to blacks in the federal government. The federal agencies began to hire thousands of black people in departments that once had been reserved for whites only. More assistance was given to black people and more programs opened up to them.

Judges were appointed who were sympathetic to civil rights. Civil rights movements began in the North to pressure stores and factories to employ blacks and unions to admit them to membership. On looking back, Stretch Johnson remembered that his salvation was to mobilize his anger constructively and make something of his life:

> There was a lot of anger in me because of what I experienced, what all black people were experiencing in those days. But it was not the kind of anger that paralyzed me. It gave me a lot of energy instead. It was a kind of anger that mobilized me, that led me to work 16–18 hours a day and make something of my life rather than lose it.

CHAPTER SEVEN

The Civilian Conservation Corps

In the early years of the depression, an estimated two million teenage boys and girls were looking for work. In normal times then, most young people went to work directly after they finished high school. Only a few went on to college. Most young men got jobs in factories or shops, and occasionally in offices or on farms. A girl graduating high school might work for a short period of time, but most girls expected to marry and raise a family. A girl who graduated and took a job as a career was deemed peculiar. The main jobs for women were in the textile mills (usually poor young women), secretarial work, beauty shops, teaching, or nursing.

After 1929, not only were there hundreds of thousands of young high school graduates seeking jobs, but many young people had quit school to find work to support themselves and their families. Gordon Parks, who survived the depression to become a great photographer, remembers arriving in New York from the Midwest to make his fortune. Unable to find a job, a creeping sense of despair began to overtake him. He remembers spending his last bit of change:

> Walking through Central Park, I decided I was fed up with poverty, hunger and New York. I tried everything I knew and failed. A winter here would send me to my grave. It was no place for a country boy to try his luck—not with so many jobless and unfriendly people. . . .
>
> I came out on 59th Street hungry and tired. There was a delicatessen with a big jar of pickles in the window. I spent a nickel on one and 15 cents for a baloney sandwich and crackers. Then I was completely broke. I went back to the edge of the park and sat underneath a tree to eat. The meat tasted good and I would take a bite of pickle after each bite of sandwich. I ate very slowly not knowing when I would eat again. I meant to save a little for later but I was so hungry, I devoured everything I bought.

What Gordon Parks was suffering in New York, others were suffering in other places throughout the country. In Chicago, Robert Ross had also reached the edge of despair:

> I had not worked in so long that the feeling had come upon me that I didn't particularly care whether or not I would ever work again. It was easy to get that way when stomachs are empty and shoes are thin. I tramped around from place to place. Everywhere I got the same answer, "Nothing doing." Then I sat around doing nothing. I could find no work. My morale was very low. I was physically and mentally broken. I had no place to go. I had no desire to go on. Then came the announcement of the CCC.

The CCC, the Civilian Conservation Corps, saved the futures—and sometimes the lives—of millions of boys and young men. The program was designed to hire teenagers and young men and organize them in work camps to improve public lands throughout the country. The idea was President Roosevelt's and grew out of two concerns of his. He wanted to help young men find jobs and he wanted to reclaim public lands. Actually, a number of European countries and several states in America had already put the idea into practice. Thirty years earlier, William James, a philosopher and psychologist, had suggested in his influential essay, "The Moral Equivalent of War," organizing a civilian army to carry out constructive environmental tasks instead of military ones. In 1932, shortly after his election as president, Franklin D. Roosevelt put James's idea to work when he announced:

One of the major jobs of the CCC was to build roads and bridges in mountain areas throughout the United States.

> I propose to create a Civilian Conservation Corps to be used in simple work, not interfering with normal employment, and confining itself to forests, the prevention of soil erosion, flood control and similar projects.

After his inauguration, the president told Congress, "I estimate that 250,000 men can be given temporary employment by early summer if you give me the authority to proceed." In March 1933, Congress authorized the creation of the CCC by passing "an act for the relief of unemployment through the performance of useful public work." The jobs would be to plant forests, build bridges, fix trucks, prevent forest fires, floods, and soil erosion, eliminate plant pests, and control tree diseases. All work was to be done on public land to avoid competition with private contractors. To be eligible, a recruit had to be between the ages of eighteen and twenty-three and pass a physical examination. Many young men were so undernourished as a result of the depression that they might have failed the examination if some of the examining doctors had not given them the benefit of the doubt. The term of enlistment was for six months and the pay was a dollar a day plus room and board. However, every recruit had to accept the condition that twenty-four dollars of his salary would be sent home to his family each month. For many families, this small amount of money meant the difference between becoming homeless and hanging on.

Roosevelt appointed Robert Fechner to head the organization. Shortly after the appointment, Roosevelt called Fechner into his office. "How long before you can start the first camp?" Roosevelt asked.

"One month," Fechner replied.

Roosevelt shook his head. "Too long."

"Two weeks?" Fechner suggested.

While the CCC did not take women recruits, there were some organizations that women could join for exercise and education.

"Good," replied the president.

Two weeks later the Civilian Conservation Corps officially opened its first camp. Soon there would be camps in every state of the Union plus Puerto Rico, the Virgin Islands, Hawaii, and Alaska. (The latter two were not yet states.) They were run by the United States Army and staffed by officers and enlisted men who applied a modified form of military discipline. Even though the recruits wore World War I uniforms, the CCC was still a peacetime organization. The army was expressly prohibited from giving the recruits military training and teaching them about war. As one officer described the recruits, "They were 'soil soldiers' who would be trained to repel the enemies of the land."

The presence of the military was intimidating to many young men. Gordon Parks remembered the military greeting he received when he first arrived:

> It was raining and mud-soaked. The sergeant, arms akimbo, legs spread in arrogant authority, slowly regarded us as if we were poisonous insects. "I give orders and see that they are carried out. Everybody understand that!?" It was quiet for a moment. The sound of the rain pelting the mud grew sharper. Suddenly, I was sorry I had come. "Okay, don't fight it," I said to myself. "Left face!" he shouted.

Not only did recruits have to measure up to the demands of their officers, they also had to measure up to the demands of their peers. Bad personal habits were not tolerated. One recruit recalled:

> If a fella didn't take a bath, we'd give him what we'd call a brushing. We'd take this fella and we'd take a big scrub brush and we'd give him a bath. Or a guy would come in and he would stink and ten guys would get him in the shower . . . we'd keep him clean.

There were a few camps for women. In those days, few people considered the fact that there were millions of young women who needed jobs and money as much as any young man. Women's needs for food, shelter, and clothing were not given serious consideration by many government officials. The belief in those days was that a woman should find a man to support her. There was not much sympathy for women who had to support themselves.

Despite the fact that there was a much higher unemployment rate for black youths, there were very few camps for them. Only one out of every seven CCC members was black. Most CCC camps were segregated and run by white officers despite the fact that the legislation creating the CCC explicitly stated that there would be no discrimination based on race, color, or creed. The law was flagrantly disobeyed. In one New Jersey camp, when the order came down for a small number of black recruits to sleep in the same tents as whites, the whites moved their belongings outside rather than share the tents with blacks.

Many communities also protested having a black CCC camp near them. In Pennsylvania, the representatives of one community wrote the president, stating:

> While disavowing any prejudice against people on account of race and color . . . [white] boys and girls should not be exposed to dangers [black] that are possible, indeed probable.

Black youths were given the worst jobs and often deliberately excluded from CCC activities. Yet despite the severe discrimination, almost 95 percent of black recruits took advantage of the education courses offered at CCC camps.

The daily routine of camp was simple. The young men rose at 5:45 A.M. and did fifteen minutes of calisthenics at 6:00. Before breakfast, the youths made their beds and cleaned their bunks. Breakfast was at 6:30. By 7:00, they were on their way to work. At 11:45, they broke for lunch and started working again one hour later. At 4:00 P.M., work ended and there was free time until 5:15, when dinner was served. After dinner, there was time for sports and leisure until 7:15, when classes began. By 10:00 P.M., lights were out. On weekends, the young men played sports and had free time to go into town, even if they didn't have much money to spend.

Gordon Parks recalled the good feeling he and so many other young men had to be working in the wilderness.

> Each morning, after breakfast, we piled onto flatbed trucks with our axes and rode to work singing. It was a good feeling to be deep in the pine-scented forest . . . , and the great trees crashing,

CCC workers removed brush areas from forests as a way to control fires.

> then booming to earth. . . . We planted trees, fought the Dutch Elm disease, built fishponds, fed wildlife, cleared timber areas of brush and made camping grounds. We had entered the camp hungry and in despair. Now we had full stomachs and hard bodies.

The change was remarkable. One youth noted that before he went to CCC camp, "I was physically and mentally broken. I had ceased to hope for the future. I had no desire to go on." He observed the defeated look of his fellow recruits. "They didn't walk, they slouched. They were stoop-shouldered, puny, whiny, grumbling about food, work, climate, clothes and commanders." After a month at the camp, everybody "strutted, their eyes clear and sparkling." The work helped transform them.

> Up in the mountains, we cut pines, and built roads, but I didn't mind any of the work, not even crushing stones with a 12-pound sledgehammer. In fact, it was good to know that I could swing a 12-pound hammer.
>
> I swung a pick until my hands were full of blisters and then my muscles toughened. The honest sweat ran over my sunburned body. I was happy in the realization that I was doing honest work building a dam for a recreation park.

The most dangerous job that the CCC youth faced was fighting fires. It was also the most glamorous, and almost everybody who joined was hoping for the opportunity to test his manhood against a forest fire. When confronted with the reality, the romance quickly faded. It was hard work, and occasionally a worker lost his life. One young man kept a diary of what it was like to fight a forest fire:

> The cry came out. "Fire! Fire!" . . .
>
> A post of red flame stretched to the sky. White smoke hung over the forest. . . . We are given a brush ax, and a lumber man's ax, a gallon of water and sandwiches. "Move up!" Before we had gone a mile, our feet and legs ceased to act . . . we march over dangerous, twisting and thickly dense brush. Lunches are thrown away to lighten the burden, feet are swollen and bloated, legs tired and we are only done with the first part. The heat is intense, unbelievable. . . .
>
> The leaves . . . are aflame. Flames shoot out of the depths of the canyon. Billows of white smoke sweep in a wide circle. . . . The camp boss approaches us. "I want some volunteers for a dangerous job." Every man volunteers. He counts off 25.
>
> The work's exhausting. Laboring under the broiling sun saps our strength. It is like the very blood is being sapped out of our

> veins. The fiery monster also brings bugs, insects, deer flies and gnats which light on our faces. There are rattlesnakes, poison oak, stinging nettles and wood ticks.
>
> "Here she comes! Here she comes!" Two men on lookout come tearing down. The conflagration is coming through a steep canyon, burning everything in its path. Rocks are loosened and tumble down the bank. Burning brands and cones are hurled through the air. The flames eat up large trunks of redwoods, consuming the bark, branches and foliage. The noise sounds like the puff, puff of a thousand locomotives. Clumps of pine burn intensely.
>
> A crew with their backs to a rocky wall are suddenly cornered by a red tongue of flame. Look out! we want to scream but the cry chokes in our throats. The men, with desperate energy, clear a space and drop to the ground. Miraculously, the flames sweep over their heads.

Separation from families and girlfriends was hard for many young men—and for those they left behind. One CCC recruit found his marriage plans canceled when his girlfriend wrote:

> We can't get married now. . . . You have to go to college. I've got to finish. We've been poor all our lives. I don't want to get stuck down somewhere with a lot of kids. Love is not enough. I want to make something of my life.

The camps gave many young men a feeling of fellowship they had never experienced before. In this pre-television age, many youths had never seen or encountered anyone from a different part of the country. It also gave some a new respect and appreciation for nature that sometimes led them to introspection. Leonard Mallory expressed these feelings in a letter to his girlfriend:

> I have met all kinds of men from all places with all kinds of stories. It is very intense, talking at night, when the camp is still and the daylife asleep. I listen at night to the sounds of birds, envying them because they can fly away. I sometimes wish that we could too, away from our lives, this country, our values and what they have done to us.

The CCC was one of the most successful of all the government programs during the depression. In the first year alone, the CCC work force created 25,000 miles of trails, installed 15,000 miles of telephone lines, built 420,000 erosion check dams, planted 98,000,000 seedlings, and worked 687,000 man-days fire-fighting. But as the thirties came to a close, young people began to find jobs and new

The CCC provided both vocational and basic education courses for recruits.

CCC recruits seemed to be different. They tended to drop out before finishing their term. In some cases, the youths were more militant and more politically aware; they refused to be bossed and staged strikes when they had grievances, just like labor unions were doing all over America. Northern and southern youths sometimes clashed over work habits and occasionally over civil rights issues. The quality of officers who ran the camps seemed to diminish toward the end, and a few were caught embezzling money. In 1941, the CCC was officially ended as young men were drafted into the armed services during World War II. But in the nine years of its existence, it accomplished much. Over two million young men had received some employment. They had improved or saved forests throughout America, built thousands of recreation camps and dams, planted millions of trees, paved thousands of roads and bridges. The CCC taught almost fifty thousand young men to read and write and enabled several thousand more to earn a high school degree.

The CCC was one of the few bright spots during the depression, even though it totally neglected women and discriminated against blacks. While it provided a shelter from the economic storm that was battering the country, it was not a long-term solution to the crisis. Every young man knew that, sooner or later, he would have to leave and return to the real world. For all of its virtues, the CCC was only an interlude in their lives. Gordon Parks expressed the underlying fear in all their minds:

> When July came, the depression still gripped the country and I knew it would still be around when our time was up in October.

CHAPTER EIGHT

Education and Other Dreams

In the 1930s, most Americans believed that to get ahead in life you needed an education. School was the door through which millions of immigrants passed to become Americans. Parents who could neither read nor write themselves insisted that their children get an education so that they could "better themselves." Children from comfortable or well-to-do homes were urged to go to college to improve their chances for success.

Just before the depression, almost 10 million children were in school throughout America. After the crash, the numbers dropped dramatically. By 1930, 3 million children between the ages of six and seventeen had dropped out. Georgia closed 1,318 schools with an enrollment of 170,790 children. In West Virginia 1,000 schools closed their doors. Arkansas's 300 schools averaged only sixty days a year of classes. Throughout the South, schools for black children either closed or cut back. White children went to school five months of the year while black children attended school an average of three months. In parts of Oklahoma, children went to school three days a

These teenagers, many of them the children of farmers, learned better ways to farm in agricultural states such as Texas.

week or less. At one point, five out of six schools in Alabama were shut down.

Not only were schools shutting down, those that stayed open often had no money to maintain the buildings and pay the teachers. New buildings were out of the question. If a window was broken and a teacher needed new textbooks, the window would stay broken and the students would do without books. One school passed a resolution not to buy new books for ten years, no matter how the world changed. There were no school supplies and few children could afford to buy notebooks and pencils. There was no money for uniforms for sports or for school teams to travel to play each other.

The parents of many black children saw education as the major means of escaping a life of poverty.

For many children, though, school was the only place they could get a decent meal. In Chicago, teachers managed to feed lunch to almost 11,000 hungry children out of their own meager resources, despite the fact that they were not being paid. "For God's sake, help us feed these children during the summer," one relief agency cried out in desperation. In New York, an estimated 20 percent of the state's schoolchildren were undernourished. In West Virginia, over 50 percent of the school-age children of miners were underweight. The quality of food was never very good in most schools.

Classes were sometimes doubled up so that one teacher was forced to do the work of two and the other teacher was fired. In some schools, salaries were cut in half. Teachers often went without salaries for long periods of time. In Chicago, a riot broke out when thousands of unpaid teachers demonstrated for the salary they had not received for almost two years between 1931 and 1933. Joined by their students and parents, the teachers marched to the city hall and invaded banks to demand their money. The police were called out and began to beat the striking teachers with clubs. (Political leaders usually found enough money to pay the police to protect them from the angry groups of the unemployed and homeless.) One teacher described her desperate search for a job as follows:

> I've been out of normal school for almost two years and have had $4.50 worth of work. Last fall I was promised a job by a school but was disappointed in the last minute by them giving it to a friend. Then I heard about . . . jobs for unemployed teachers and I registered for work right away. . . . I was to be put on a library project at $22.50. The next day I was taken ill with measles which put me out again. Then I started answering advertisements for girls in our paper. I wrote for housework, practical nurse, factory work, anything I could find but nothing came of it.

One Oklahoma woman remembered her parents pushing her to go to school during the dust bowl days.

> Mom and Dad were determined we kids were going to school. It didn't matter if there was dust storms, black blizzards, white blizzards, depression or what have you. We was to go and that's all there was to it. Actually, I didn't mind so much 'cause we had a horse and carriage and Mom would let us hitch her up and ride to school. It was six miles away. We gave as many kids rides as we could so we were very popular.

The depression affected school enrollment in contradictory ways. In many areas, where work was hard to find, teenagers stayed in school

These Oklahoma children drove to school using this horse and buggy.

because there was no place else for them to go. As a result, many classes were packed full with students who, in normal times, would have entered the work force. However, many children no longer could afford to go to school. Some didn't have carfare; others lacked clothes or books, or lived too far away to walk. A fourteen-year-old Kentucky girl was one of many who wrote of her plight to Mrs. Roosevelt, the president's wife, and asked for help.

> I was a freshman at the Paintsville High School but had to quit going on account of the depression. The school was about seven miles away. When I was going I had to get up about 5:30 every morning. . . . My parents worked hard to keep me in school but since we lived on a farm and could sell nothing, I had to quit school.

Sometimes the school was too far away to walk and students could not afford the bus fare, even when it was inexpensive. A fourteen-year-old Illinois girl wrote:

> I want to enter high school but I find it very hard. . . . The school is about six miles away. The bus fare is not free but seventy-five cents a week besides books. If my bus fare were paid I could easily go. . . . You are my only hope. My father is gone for five years and we don't know where.

Many teenagers were ashamed to go to school because they lacked clothes. Farm children sometimes wore clothes that their mothers made out of burlap bags that once contained grain. Two brothers went to school on alternate days because they only had one pair of shoes between them. A sixteen-year-old Michigan girl wrote Mrs. Roosevelt:

> I am a high school girl and I must quit school because I am not dressed as other girls are. My clothes are all so shabby from my dress to my shoes. Mrs. Roosevelt, would you kindly look among your things and see if there isn't something you can send me. Please don't let my parents find out that I wrote you asking you for help. I am decent and respectable and you know how some people are. They would laugh at me if they knew I wrote and asked you for old dresses.

Proms were especially important to teenagers, despite the fact that they might seem trivial under the circumstances. For many teenagers, the prom was the most important social event of their life until marriage. Many teenagers were anguished that their parents could not afford to buy them the clothes they needed. One seventeen-year-old high school girl explained why she needed help after saving nineteen dollars to buy "a beautiful blue evening dress and silver, high heel sandals":

> Oh, the joy of dreaming of all this [evening clothes]. I was determined to make the other girls turn and stare at me for the first time instead of having them remark about my poor clothes. But then my baby brother took sick with a bad cold and then we had to have the Dr. and then send him to the san [sanatorium]. Well, I gave all my money . . . to help pay for the hospital bill. Oh! to see Dad and mother so happy was worth more than all the evening frocks in the world. Donny is getting along wonderful . . . the result of wonderful care. Oh! How sorry I am I didn't have more money to give.
>
> Well, I just couldn't ask Dad because it would only make him blue that he couldn't help me. Don't you know of some young girl who wears a size 16 dress and a size 5 slipper who would be kind enough to lend it to me for the night of April 22. Oh! I would take such care of them and send them back the next day.

Many children's education suffered because they could not afford to buy books or supplies they needed for school. One fourteen-year-old boy pleaded for a donation of books because "I love to learn." A young New Mexican girl asked for a typewriter: "I just love to study and all my wishes are to be a stenographer but my parents are very poor. . . ." A Minnesota farm girl wrote:

> I have done a boy's work ever since I was five years old. This week I have been breaking land with a sulky plow and three mules. Is there some way I can hear music and talks and news outside my very small world? I have so little pleasures and pastimes. We are just poor renters on a farm and there is no money for a radio or the books I like to read.

A New York City girl pleading "my dad is completely broke" made up a list of books she needed to continue school.

First Spanish Course—Hills and Ford
Correct English—Tanner
Modern Biography—Hyde
New Plain Geometry—Durrel
Second Latin Book—Ullman and Henry

Some children of the rich also found their education disrupted and their sheltered lives turned upside down. Phyllis Lorimer described what happened to her when the depression struck her family to author Studs Terkel, for his book *Hard Times:*

> When it happened, I was at boarding school which I loved. It was the best boarding school in California at that time. I was about to be president of the student body and very proud of myself. Suddenly, I couldn't get any pencils and I went to the principal's office to find out why. She was embarrassed because we were old friends. She said, "I'm sorry but the bills haven't been paid." She complimented me by saying, "Were there scholarships, you could have it." . . . I was mortified beyond belief.

For the most part, in the thirties, it was taken for granted that if a sacrifice had to be made in the family, it was the women who would make it. Thus, Phyllis Lorimer was taken out of school while her brother stayed in college:

> My brother was still in Dartmouth where he was fortunate enough not to know what was going on at home. Whatever money there was was used to keep brother at Dartmouth. He lived extremely well . . . with a socialite friend in a house with a manservant while . . . we were living on a form of relief. We had cans of tinned bully beef. And we had the gas turned off. My mother was an engaging lady who made everything a picnic. We

> cooked on an electric corn popper. When there was money, she'd buy me a china doll instead of vegetables.

Not only did teenagers have to abandon school, they also had to give up their dreams of a better life through other means of learning. Many children with limited means had great ambitions to become an artist or writer to escape their poverty. "I am greatly in love with my music and I have my heart set on making my future in it," one seventeen-year-old girl wrote, requesting a grant that was denied. A nineteen-year-old Chicago youth also asked for a grant, believing he had the talent and ambition to be an opera singer. He was then selling newspapers for a dollar a day to help support his parents. A black teenager desired to go to college to become a journalist, a subject which she found "fascinating and charming."

Many young people had more limited ambitions. They wanted jobs as auto mechanics or hairdressers, or to open their own small businesses. A seventeen-year-old girl wrote:

> I am a cripple girl and can't do any outside work. I have been cripple since I was one year and seven months. I want to take a course in hooked rug making. I don't want to be idle. . . . You don't know how it is to want to buy things that you need and can't because you haven't the money.

In the 1930s, many young people struggled to stay in college, even though a college degree was no longer a guarantee of a job. (It was estimated that during the depression, several hundred thousand college graduates were unemployed.) Some students lived in broken-down cars. One student on the verge of collapse from malnutrition was found to be feeding himself on only fifty cents a week. One former student at Berkeley in California recalled:

> There were kids who didn't have a place to sleep, huddling under bridges on the campus. I had a scholarship but at times I didn't even have food. The meals were often three candy bars.

Some students found ingenious ways of surviving. One group chipped in and bought a cow and chickens to ensure having enough milk and eggs. Some went into business for themselves and offered all kinds of services as dog washers, maids, laundresses, barbers, and hairdressers. One young man held twenty-seven jobs at the same time ranging from scorekeeper at baseball games to editor in chief of the college newspaper.

The federal government did try to help students stay in college by providing some financial assistance. Some seventy-five thousand students eventually received government aid through the National Youth Act, a bill designed to create jobs for young people and provide limited financial help for others. Students received about twenty dollars a month in assistance to supplement other income. The amounts were always small, but during the depression, people learned how to make a little bit go a long way.

Not all students had to struggle. There were still many young people whose parents did not lose either their jobs or their money. Many of these students were resented for their insensitivity. One student who did have to struggle recalled:

> . . . a lot of the kids were well-heeled. I still have a resentment against the fraternity boys and the sorority girls with their cashmere sweaters and the pearls. . . .

The depression took its toll on the spirit of the young. For many, there was little chance that even the simplest of their youthful dreams would be realized. A nineteen-year-old college girl on the verge of despair wrote:

> I feel a bitterness I myself cannot understand. . . . I wonder sometimes why I go on living. What is the use of it and . . . why do I work so hard to get ahead of what I was born into?

But many managed to survive and accept the hard times they endured with a hopeful and even, at times, a cheerful outlook. A fourteen-year-old girl expressed her feelings by writing to a friend:

> Yes, we are poor as far as money is concerned but as for happiness? Don't you know, we are millionaires?

CHAPTER NINE

Growing Up Rich

It didn't take much money to be rich in 1929. If a man earned $6,000 a year he was among the top 5 percent of earners in the United States and could live quite well. A nest egg of $115,000 conservatively invested could earn $5,000 a year in interest, which meant that the investor wouldn't have to work for a living. And because taxes were low, most people kept most of the money they earned.

But the truly rich were, of course, the millionaires. There were the famous wealthy families in the United States such as the Rockefellers, Astors, Vanderbilts, and Mellons, all of whom made their fortunes in nineteenth-century America. They were considered the "old money." Then there were the newly rich, like Joseph Kennedy, the father of the future president of the United States, who made his fortune in bootlegging and the movies. When the crash came, most of these men survived. They had the good sense to get out before the collapse; or if they lost money, they had enough invested wisely to cushion their fall. Many wealthy families continued their lives as if the depression never happened. Women were photographed attending fancy balls in dresses that cost as much as ten thousand dollars to make. One woman had her picture taken in a dress made from thousand-dollar bills. Millionaires would throw parties that cost fifty thousand dollars or more. Many of their children were not even aware of the depression. "I don't recall ever seeing bread lines in my city," one woman from St. Louis stated. "I wasn't even aware of the depression until I saw a group of homeless men huddled together under a bridge." Another remembered her first childhood encounter with the sufferings caused by the depression:

Many children of wealthy parents were not affected by the depression and went on to college. But a large number of students worked their way through.

> I remember going to the park with my governess . . . holding her hand. . . . There was a shanty town. Like a Hooverville. It was for me the most palpable memory of the other side of the tracks. . . .
>
> For years, I felt exempt. I grew up feeling immune and exempt from circumstances. . . . I never felt adversity. . . . I never saw a real breadline except in the movies.

Some of the rich who lost their fortunes did so because they were greedy. They had made fortunes on paper but instead of taking their winnings, they not only invested what they had made, but they continued to borrow more money to invest. When the stock market tumbled, they lost everything, including their self-esteem. In some cases, the desire to make money had become a sickness. One wealthy woman in a small town continued to invest after the crash despite the advice of her lawyer and banker. First, she lost the securities her husband had left her when he died. Then she lost her savings. Then she mortgaged her home and invested the proceeds to recoup her losses. At the end, she lost everything and was completely destitute, living on charity.

Many parents who lost everything felt that they had failed their children. It was painful for them to deny them things that they had been able to give them in good times. Enid Wilson was, in her words, a child of "landed gentry," who lived in a seven-bedroom house in the Midwest. She was used to a life of comfort and ease and thought her family rich. Her father used to give her little presents. One day, the presents stopped. Strange people visited the house and spoke with her father behind closed doors. Then everything ended:

> When the crash came, my father lost everything . . . money, farm, house, everything. I remember waking up one morning.

> Everybody was screaming. I got up and looked out the window. Mother was running and my sister was yelling, "Daddy is hanging in the barn."

Adele Buschmeyer was thirteen when the crash came, the daughter of a wealthy man who lost all his money. She had been raised in luxury in Columbia, South Carolina, in a big house, with servants to wait on her, and all the dolls, toys, and dresses she wanted; she attended the best private schools. Adele remembers that she thought that her family "was ahead of everybody else because we had two bathrooms while most people had one." When the crash came, everyone was caught by surprise.

> My father had invested heavily in the stock market and when the Crash came, he lost most of his money. But the worst part was that the real estate company in which my father was vice-president and treasurer became bankrupt. This was a terrible thing, because not only did my father lose his own money, others who invested with him also lost their money. My father felt disgraced. He was very depressed. He tried to borrow money from monied people. It was crushing when they said no. There was one particular man that everybody knew had lots of money and father made an appointment to see this man. I remember that he wanted to look his best and his coat had become threadbare. And momma and I ripped it all apart and pressed all the pieces and put it back together with the inside out—and daddy had a new coat! It didn't do him any good though. Father asked the man for one hundred dollars and the man said "no" and my father came home and cried. That's the only time I ever saw him crying. He was so depressed. And mother confided in me—I was only 13 at the time—that he might commit suicide. That's what a lot of men were doing in those days. They couldn't face the future or

> they wanted to cash in on their life insurance to support their families.

To cut down on expenses, Adele's parents gave up their nine-room house and let all the servants go. For the first time in her life, Adele had to make her own bed and clean her own room. Nor did she know what happened to those who had taken care of her throughout her childhood after they were dismissed. Her mother took in a boarder in their new house, which helped to meet the rent. While Adele's parents tried to protect the children at first, eventually they had to take her out of an exclusive girls' junior high school she attended:

> They also had the braces on my teeth removed because Daddy could no longer afford to pay for them. I stopped taking music lessons. I had to give up my dancing lessons. I wanted to take art lessons and I couldn't do that. Daddy had wanted me to go to Wellesley College when I graduated high school—it was one of the best colleges for women in America—and I could forget about that. What upset my parents most was the fact that I had to go to public school. Actually, that made me very happy. The private school I was in was very, very tough—I was always trying to keep up. When I got to public school, it was so much easier. I got on the honor roll. I was also going to school with boys—which was something new and exciting in my life.

Many of Adele's friends' families were in the same boat that she was. Their parents had also been adversely affected by the depression. Everyone began to economize. "In junior high school, I only had two plaid skirts. Every evening, I would take them out and press them to take the bulge out of the back to make them nice and new."

Social life for young people also changed dramatically. Before the depression, a young wealthy southern girl could look forward to evenings filled with parties and balls. "That changed," Adele recalls:

> Dates were fun because you didn't have a lot of money. Our main entertainment was movies. Going to get a Coke somewhere. If you bought a bowl of potato chips and a Coke, that was enough.

Parents often tried to shield their children as long as they could from what was happening. They would pretend everything was all right until, one day, their children discovered the truth. One college girl recalled:

> It was my junior year in college. I came home and found the phone disconnected. This was when I realized the world was falling apart. When I finished school I couldn't avoid facing the fact that we didn't have a cook anymore, we didn't have a cleaning woman anymore. I'd seen dust under the beds which is something I had never seen before. I knew the curtains weren't as clean as they used to be. Things began to look a little shabby.
>
> I remember how embarrassed I was when friends came from out of town to see me because sometimes they'd say, "We want a drink of water," and we didn't have any ice. We didn't have an electric refrigerator and we couldn't afford to buy ice. There would be those frantic arrangements of running out to the drugstore to get Coca Cola with crushed ice and there would be this embarrassing delay and I can remember how hot my face was.

Some children went from riches to rags almost overnight without any preparation for the drastic change. Phyllis Lorimer remembered how, by day, she kept up the appearances of her family's former wealth while at night she faced the grim reality of her poverty.

> I had come from this terribly wealthy family, with cousins that still had so much that even during the Depression, they didn't

> lose it. Suddenly I had four great white horses . . . given to me by my cousins, I was a very good horsewoman, I rode all the shows . . . and then went home to canned . . . beef at night.

Like many young rich girls of her day, Phyllis was not trained to do anything really useful in life.

> Having gone to a proper lady's finishing school, I didn't know how to do anything. I spoke a little bad French and knew enough to stand up when an older person came into the room. As far as anything else was concerned, I was unequipped.

There were many families who, although not millionaires, had achieved the middle-class success promised in the American Dream. They had worked hard and prospered and then lost everything. One Chicago woman remembered how the depression affected her and her family when she was a teenager. She had grown up in comfort, but her family's fortunes were reversed as she entered high school.

> I remember all of a sudden we had to move. My father lost his job and we had to move into a double garage. The landlord didn't charge us rent for seven years. We had a coal stove and we had to each take turns, the three of us kids, to warm our legs. It was awfully cold when you opened those garage doors. We would sleep with rugs and blankets over the top of us. And dress underneath the covers.
>
> In the morning, we'd get out and get some snow and put it on the stove and wash around our faces. Never the neck or anything. Put two pairs of socks on each hand and two pairs of socks on our feet and long underwear and lace up with Goodwill shoes. Off we'd walk, three, four miles to school.
>
> My father could always get something to feed us kids. We lived for about three months on candy pods, little square chocolate things. We had them melted in milk. He worked part time

> in a Chinese restaurant. We lived on fried noodles. He went to delivering Corn Flake samples. We lived on Corn Flakes, Rice Krispies, till they came out our ears.
>
> My mother was raised in a lace curtain Irish family and went to a finishing school. We had napkin rings even during the Depression. . . . It was status with my mother . . . my father used to call her "Queenie." She always had grandiose ideas.
>
> My mother always picked a school where the other children were far better off than we were. She worked at a cleaning store to manage the tuition and books. We could have gone to a free public school.
>
> I finished high school and sort of got engaged. I thought maybe if I got married, I could eat hamburgers and hot-dogs, have a ball, play the guitar and sing. Anything would be better than coming home and sleeping on the floor.

Surprisingly enough, many children were able to withstand adversity much better than their parents. One man recalled how his father used to take him and his brother out every weekend and spend four or five dollars amusing them. When the depression came, his father still tried to keep up appearances even though he lost his business. Finally, it was he and his brother who told their parents not to spend money on them until "daddy's business is better."

The sense of guilt often made the fathers of children strive twice as hard to pull themselves out of their difficulty. Adele Buschmeyer remembered the price her father paid for that:

> By 1937, my father recovered. He had built a beautiful new home for us. He did this in five years. And at that time mother said to me that father was a broken man. And I could see it. I could see it in his face and his whole body. He was a broken man. I really believed her. One year later, in 1938, he died of cancer.

CHAPTER TEN

What Happened

In 1929, Albert Wiggins, the powerful chairman of Chase Bank, was asked during a congressional hearing, "Is the capacity for human suffering unlimited?" "I think so," was his unfeeling reply. But the capacity for human suffering during the depression was not unlimited, as the following story from a Youngstown, Ohio, newspaper in 1931 illustrated:

> Out of work for two years, Charles Wayne, age 57, father of ten children, stood on the Spring Common bridge this morning, watching hundreds of other persons on their way to work. Then he took off his coat, folded it carefully, and jumped into the swirling Mahoney river. . . .
>
> "We were about to lose our home," sobbed Mrs. Wayne. "And the gas and electric companies had threatened to shut off service."

The depression lasted ten long years and many people were broken by it. Tragedy followed upon tragedy. Suicide rates increased. Despite the myth that most suicides were those who lost all their money on Wall Street, the reality was that most suicides were committed by men and women who had lost their jobs, their savings, and their homes. A seventy-two-year-old man laid off without a pension and savings waited until his wife went out shopping one day and then turned on the gas. Three days after his funeral, his wife followed him. After he had foolishly bankrupted his company, the president of the Studebaker automobile company killed himself so his family could collect his $750,000 life insurance policy. A dentist and his wife committed suicide together when his patients could no longer afford to pay him, leaving just enough money with a friend for their burial. A man who was seen stealing a loaf of bread for his children ran into his house and hung himself in his basement before the police arrived to arrest him.

The greatest tragedy for many children was that the depression robbed them of the opportunity to have a normal childhood and a decent life.

Not all the tragedies ended in death. Many people were broken or beaten down, never to recover; young people were forced to give up their dreams for careers or loves they might otherwise have had if the depression had not happened. Some people wound up in mental wards because they could no longer deal with the stress. Others became ill with the two most dreaded diseases of the day, polio and tuberculosis, which were brought about, in part, by poor nourishment and unsanitary conditions. There were millions of cases of malnutrition and undernourishment, especially among children in the South, where the main diet consisted of pinto beans, potatoes, and occasionally "white meat"—the name given to pork belly meat. The average weight of young people throughout the United States dropped 12 percent.

The depression also saw its share of people rebelling. There were hundreds of incidents throughout the country in which people broke into stores and warehouses and took what they needed. In Arkansas, five hundred armed men entered a town with guns and pitchforks and threatened to take food from stores unless it was given to them in some other way without cost. In Oklahoma, a small mob raided a grocery store and removed all the food from its shelves. In Indiana, fifteen hundred men stormed a company and demanded jobs and had to be chased away by police. In Minnesota, crowds broke into stores and helped themselves to food. In Texas, when the manager of a relief depot was found to be stealing government food meant for poor black farmers and then reselling it, three white men entered the store and told the manager that if he didn't start distributing the food right away, they'd blow his head off.

People also rebelled by stealing. Children stole a great deal, often with the encouragement of their parents. In those days, bottles of milk were delivered to homes and left on the doorstep. Children (and adults) stole them. Children would also steal food from grocery stores, vegetables from farmers' fields, supplies from delivery trucks, and clothing from shops. Most of what they stole was for their families and themselves. Relatively few stole money, although sometimes they sold what they stole. But the underlying motive was survival. The reason most people stole was to stay alive.

> "My folks didn't mind if I stole," one man said, recalling his youth, as long as it was something we really needed. But if I stole for the fun of it or because it was something I just wanted, I'd get the stuffings knocked out of me if my father found out.

Many children had to give up any thought of presents during the depression years. Younger children wrote letters to the president and Mrs. Roosevelt asking for gifts for themselves or others. One child wanted seven dollars to buy a bicycle "I want so bad but my people are too poor to afford." Another asked for fifty dollars "to buy a mule so we can raise something to eat as we live so hard and don't get scarcely any clothes." Another request was for fifteen dollars to buy a "Model T Ford." A thirteen-year-old Massachusetts girl wanted money "to buy gifts for my parents because I cannot bear to see them suffer so much, they are in debt to most everybody."

Christmas was an especially hard time for children. One ten-year-old wrote:

> On Christmas eve I waited for Santa Claus but my momma said the chimney was blocked and he couldn't come so I had a poor Christmas. I lost my daddy when I was two years old. . . . all the children talk about how many presents Santa has brought them and I feel so bad I have nothing to say. . . .

Another lonely child wrote,

> I am a girl eleven years of age. I have no mother and no father. I haven't any toys to play with. I wanted some toys before my parents died but they didn't have the money.

Another offered Mrs. Roosevelt the chance for untold riches for himself and for her:

> How would you like to be a partner with us in the gold and silver mines? My father is a miner and prospector. I am 15 years old and trying to get a good education. We have no money to live on so we cannot go to the mountains. We will give you 1/4 interest in all the mineral claims we discover if you finance the project.

One thing that helped children survive the deprivations they suffered was the community feeling that developed. Many people were in the same boat. Those who were migrating from the dust bowls of the Midwest to California were continually sharing their food and rides, and burying the dead of fellow migrants they met on the way. Stretch Johnson recalled the feelings of fellowship that permeated the black community:

> There was a cohesion of the entire community where if one person had a job, he would invite his neighbors to sit at the table. And they shared food. Doors were never locked. Doors were wide open. And kids would go from household to household. Whenever somebody had a big dinner, they invited whoever was hungry to the table. There was a lot of that kind of sharing that made the poverty that much less oppressive.

There were many who took the worst that the depression had to offer, suffered, yet survived and became, in their judgment, better people for it. Adele Buschmeyer saw good come out of it for herself, even though it cost her father his life:

> Being in the depression sounds very bad. But frankly, I'm glad I'm a depression child because it helped me to cope with my own life in later years.

Viola Cooper remembered how people dug in and wouldn't give up:

> We just couldn't throw up our hands and quit. You never do know what life is going to bring you. We had to have faith. We just had to keep on keeping on for sure. And that's what we did and a lot of people did that, went through the dust bowl, the depression days.

And Bill Bailey drew parallels between his life as a teenage hobo and the lives of other young people he now sees around him:

> I would hate to live it all over again. I don't think I could jump into a box car. I don't think I could stand the stink of a cattle car again or the humiliation of bumming somebody for a meal, or walking into a restaurant and telling them that I would do the dishes for nothing for a hamburger. There are young people in this country today that are going through the same thing we went through. And like I found, there are still real good people in this country that are concerned about them, that will give a helping hand, that will pick you up out of the gutter and help straighten you out . . . if you ask them.

Bibliography

Agee, James. *Let Us Now Praise Famous Men*. Boston: Houghton Mifflin, 1941.

Allen, Frederick Lewis. *Since Yesterday: The 1930s in America*. New York: Harper & Row, 1939.

Bird, Caroline. *The Invisible Scar: The Great Depression and What It Did to American Life, from Then Until Now*. New York: David McKay & Co., 1956.

Hurt, R. Douglas. *The Dust Bowl: An Agricultural and Social History*. Chicago: Nelson-Hall, 1981.

Klingaman, William. *1929, the Year of the Great Crash*. New York: Harper & Row, 1989.

Leuchtenburg, William. *Franklin D. Roosevelt and the New Deal, 1932–1940*. New York: Harper & Row, 1963.

Markowitz, Gerald, and David Rosner. *Slaves of the Depression*. Ithaca, N.Y.: Cornell University Press, 1987.

McElvaine, Robert S., ed. *Down and Out in the Great Depression: Letters from the Forgotten Man*. Chapel Hill: University of North Carolina Press, 1983.

———. *The Great Depression, 1929–1941*. New York: New York Times, 1984.

McWilliams, Carey. *Farmers in the Field*. Hamden, Conn.: Archon, 1969.

Parks, Gordon. *A Choice of Weapons*. St. Paul, Minn.: Historical Society Press, 1986.

Schlesinger, Arthur M. *The Age of Roosevelt: Vol. 1. The Crisis of the Old Order*. Boston: Houghton Mifflin, 1956.

———. *The Age of Roosevelt: Vol. 2. The Coming of the New Deal*. Boston: Houghton Mifflin, 1956.

———. *The Age of Roosevelt: Vol. 3. The Politics of Upheaval*. Boston: Houghton Mifflin, 1956.

Stein, Walter J. *California and the Dust Bowl Migration*. Westport, Conn.: Greenwood Press, 1973.

Terkel, Studs. *Hard Times: An Oral History of the Great Depression*. New York: Pantheon Books, 1986.

Index